'NIDS

RAY GARTON

ISBN 978-1-63789-670-9
Macabre Ink is an imprint of Crossroad Press Publishing

For information address Crossroad Press at 141 Brayden Dr., Hertford, NC 27944
www.crossroadpress.com

Cover art and design by David Dodd

First Crossroad Press Edition - 2023

For Dawn

PART ONE
An Unidentified Animal

One

The explosion took place on a clear, cool spring night that smelled of honeysuckle, beneath a bright crescent moon.

It was the first time seventeen-year-old Rodney Lepke had brought Heidi Stokes to the place known as Lovers' Lookout. It had been a make-out spot for generations. Rodney's parents had come to Lovers' Lookout when *they* were in high school. Everyone in Hope Valley—the natives, anyway—had been there at least once. To get there, you had to drive a short way out of town and up Creasey Hill Road. It was a dirt road riddled with potholes that led up to the top of the hill where the Creasey family used to live decades ago. The family had left town after the house burned down long ago. Now, the road was used only by teenagers looking for a place to park. Halfway up the hill, a turnout provided a nice view. Half of Hope Valley was visible from Lovers' Lookout. From there, you could watch a movie on the big drive-in screen at the northern end of town. North of the town, less than a mile from the turnout where they were parked, just beyond a patch of woods, was BioGenTech, Inc. It was a blocky rectangular gray building that had been erected eight years ago. It was a bit of an eyesore sticking out of the sprawling green woods, but it had provided a lot of jobs for residents of Hope Valley and nearby Newbury and Ridgeton.

The crickets were so loud that night, they were clearly audible above the radio playing a song by Evanescence.

Rodney had not yet made the first move. He and Heidi had only started dating a couple of days before.

"I've never been up here before," Heidi said.

She had moved to Hope Valley only a week ago. Her father worked for the Forest Service and had been transferred there from Southern California.

"It's called Lovers' Lookout," Rodney said.

Rodney's white 1972 Mustang convertible had bucket seats, but he reached back and took a big pillow from the back seat and placed it between the buckets. Heidi scooted over a little closer to him.

"Is that why you brought me up here?" Heidi said. "To have your way with me?"

"Well, yeah, I was kinda hoping."

She laughed. "Are you nervous, or something?"

"Nervous? Why?"

"I don't know, you seem … kinda stiff."

"Yeah, well … maybe a little."

"Don't be." She leaned over and kissed him on the lips. It was a brief, gentle kiss and her breath was minty. She pulled back a little and smiled. "I don't bite," she whispered.

Rodney put his arm around her, pulled her to him and kissed her. It lasted longer this time. Their tongues met as he passed his hand over her back.

The song on the radio changed, but they were no longer listening to it.

Rodney put both arms around her and she scooted closer to him. When they separated for a breath, he kissed her cheek, then her neck. He was afraid to appear too eager, so he tried to hold back a little, although it wasn't easy.

Heidi was a beautiful girl—long dark hair; deep, soulful brown eyes; full and pouty lips; and a body that made guys stop and gawk at her like lobotomy cases. And she was with Rodney. He found that more than a little surprising.

The day Heidi had come to Hope Valley High School, Rodney had been walking by the principal's office when he'd heard his name called. Mrs. Kirtney, the principal, was standing in the office doorway with Heidi. She'd called Rodney over, introduced him to Heidi, and asked if he'd be willing to take her under his wing and show her around the school for her first day. Had that not happened, Rodney doubted they would have gotten together. Heidi was the kind of girl who was immediately taken in by the popular crowd, of which Rodney was not a member. But Heidi hadn't known that. He'd been nervous at first, but after showing her around that first day, he'd become quite comfortable with her. He'd made her laugh a lot that first day and she'd actually seemed to like him. They'd been together ever since.

They kissed for a while as the radio played and the Mustang's windows fogged up. She nibbled on his ear and he stifled a laugh.

"What's funny?" she said.

"That tickles."

"Oh, you're ticklish, huh?"

She tickled his ribs with one hand. Rodney wiggled and laughed as he tried to push her hand away.

"You've got it bad," she said as she tickled him with the other hand.

Light oozed through the foggy windows as another car pulled up. It was closely followed by another.

"We're not alone," Heidi said.

"Yeah, we are." As he kissed her again, he tickled her ribs, but she didn't react.

"I'm not ticklish," she said, her lips still touching his. "Not there, anyway."

"Where?"

"I'm not telling. You've gotta find out for yourself."

But Rodney wasn't interested in tickling. He passed his hands over her body as their kissing intensified.

Two

The first of the two cars to join Rodney and Heidi at Lovers' Lookout was a blue 2000 Volkswagen Beetle. Alan Burgess was at the wheel, and his girlfriend Natalie Williams sat in the passenger seat. As soon as Alan killed the engine, he and Natalie got out of the car, pulled their seats forward, and got in the back seat.

"Rodney's here," Alan said.

"Yeah, I saw his car. You think he's with that new girl?"

"I don't know who else he'd be with. I don't know who's in the other car."

"Yeah, I don't recognize it, either," Natalie said. "Is the beer cold?"

"Cold enough."

A six-pack of Coors was on the floorboard behind the driver's seat. Alan handed one of the bottles to Natalie and took one for himself. The caps made little *phut* sounds when they were unscrewed.

"A toast," Alan said.

"To what?"

"To, uh ..." He shrugged. "I dunno."

Natalie laughed as they touched their bottles together, then drank.

"I hope you've got some Binaca, or something," Natalie said. "If my mom smells beer on my breath again, she's gonna freak."

"I've got Binaca and Tic Tacs in the glove compartment."

"Good."

They drank some more, then Alan put an arm around her shoulders and pulled her to him.

"Wait till we finish our beer," Natalie said.

"What're you, an alcoholic?"

"No, I just wanna finish my beer. I mean, you don't want beer spilled in your car, do you? The smell sticks around."

"Can I at least feel you up?" he said.

"If you want, sure."

Natalie drank her beer as Alan slid a hand beneath her pale green sweater. She wasn't wearing a bra and he found one of her breasts, cupped it in his hand. He ran his thumb back and forth over her nipple, which quickly became hard.

Natalie laughed and reached down between his legs. "You're already hard."

"When I'm around you, I'm *always* hard. When was the last time I told you you've got the best tits in Hope Valley?"

"I think it was last night on the phone."

"Finish that beer." He pulled his hand out from under her sweater. He put the beer bottle to his mouth and tilted it back, gulped the rest of the beer. He put the empty bottle back in the cardboard six-pack.

"If I did that, I'd belch until breakfast," Natalie said.

Alan took her beer away from her and gulped it down. "There. You're done with your beer. Take off that sweater."

"You're always in such a *hurry*."

"I can't help it if you drive me crazy."

"I'm not responsible for that." She pulled the sweater off over her head.

Alan's eyes drank in her breasts for a moment, then he leaned forward and put his mouth on one of them. They were round and full and pert, with pale nipples.

Alan and Natalie had been together since November. They'd met on the yearbook committee and had been unable to keep their hands off of each other ever since.

"Take off the skirt," Alan said as he unbuttoned his shirt.

"Why? I'm not wearing any underwear."

"You're not? Oh, shit, you make me crazy."

Natalie laughed. "I swear, you are *so* easy to please."

Three

In the battered old silver Toyota Corolla that had come in behind Alan and Natalie, Brandon Carr lit a joint. He inhaled the smoke and held it in his lungs.

"Do you, like, *have* to smoke that?" Tiffany Huff said.

He waited a moment, then exhaled slowly. "I don't *have* to," he said, "but I *want* to. I was hopin' you'd have some, too."

"Well ... maybe a little. But if I smell from that stuff when I get home, my parents are gonna, like, shit fire, or something."

Brandon handed the joint to her. She took a drag on it, held it, exhaled.

"Why'd you bring me out here?" she said.

"Just wanted to talk."

"We could've done that at, like, Denny's, or something." She handed the joint back to him.

He held up the joint and said, "We couldn't do *this* at Denny's." He took another hit.

"I'm serious, Brandon, why'd we come here?"

He exhaled smoke slowly, then said, "I've missed you."

"We're over, I told you. What happened the night of the winter dance—that was, like, a mistake. A fluke."

"It was enough to make me miss you."

"Look, Brandon, we don't have anything in common, okay?"

He smiled and said, "We had plenty in common the night of the winter dance."

"You weren't even supposed to, like, *be* there. You dropped out of school."

Brandon and Tiffany had dated for a while a couple of years ago, but she'd broken it off. She'd thought he was running with the wrong crowd and knew he'd get into trouble sooner or later. He did, several times, first at school, then with the police. Among other things, he'd been caught playing mailbox baseball with a couple of friends. Since then, his problems had escalated. He'd gotten caught breaking into a gas station convenience store late one night just to steal some snacks, got a few speeding tickets and began to drink a lot. By the time he dropped out of school last year, he'd worked up quite a list of offenses. Tiffany knew he had problems at home; his mother had died a few years ago, and his dad was an abusive drunk. But while he had her pity, there was no way she could start seeing him again. Tiffany was a cheerleader and Brandon simply did not fit in with her group of friends.

He'd shown up at the winter dance, where Tiffany had gotten into a fight with her date. Brandon had taken her for a drive afterward and they'd ended up at Lovers' Lookout, where they'd had sex.

If he's so wrong for you, Tiffany thought, then what are you doing here with him now? You could've told him no.

The truth was, Brandon made her melt inside. He had dark hair that fell to his shoulders, a narrow face with an olive complexion, nice cheekbones, such kissable lips, and eyes that seemed to look inside her. He was tall, with sleek, defined muscles. Even his voice was sexy—low and deep, with a touch of gruffness. It made her angry to admit it to herself, but she found it hard to tell him no.

"C'mon, admit it," Brandon said. "You'd like to drop out with me, but your parents would never let you."

"No way. What do you expect to do with, like, your *life* if you don't go to school?"

"Something more interesting than going to school."

"I'm sorry, Brandon, but you're just not right for me."

He smiled. "Yes I am. And you know it. Otherwise, you wouldn't be here now, you would've told me to get lost."

"I'm not the type of person who, like, tells people to get lost. Besides, I'm worried about you. I heard the sheriff found you drunk in the cemetery a couple weeks ago."

Brandon shrugged. "No big deal."

"Well, I'm just … concerned."

"Why don't you be concerned about this." He pulled her toward him, put his mouth over hers, licked her lips and pressed his tongue between them as he pressed her hand over his erection.

Tiffany wanted to protest, to push away and insist that he take her home. But she didn't want it enough to actually do it. She went limp in Brandon's arms and became immersed in his kiss.

That was when the explosion occurred.

Four

It was so loud—a tremendous, gut-punching *ka-BAP!*—it made Rodney jump and pull away from Heidi. They both looked out the windshield and saw the flames in the valley below.

"What the hell was that?" Rodney said.

"Oh, my god," Heidi said in a whisper. "It's BioGenTech."

"Are you sure?"

Heidi opened her door and got out of the car.

Rodney turned off the radio, got out and went around the rear of the car to join her. They walked to the top of the bank that sloped steeply down into the woods.

"You're right," he said. "Oh, shit, is your dad working tonight?"

"No, he only works during the day. I don't know how many people they have there during the night."

Black smoke roiled upward from BioGenTech, and flames burned with orange halos at the southern end of the building.

Car doors closed and Rodney turned to see three people walking toward them from the other two cars. He recognized them—Alan, Natalie, and Brandon—and noticed that someone remained in the Toyota.

"Is that BioGenTech?" Brandon said. He had a cigarette between the thumb and forefinger of his right hand.

"Yeah," Rodney said.

"I hope nobody was hurt," Heidi said.

"What exactly do they *do* there, anyway?" Alan said. "I've never really heard what goes on in that place."

Rodney said, "Medical research, genetic stuff. I *think*, anyway. They made a big deal about the place when they built it about five years ago, but they were never too clear on exactly what they do there."

Brandon said. "Wonder what blew up."

Another explosion cracked the night open and a ball of fire rose from the building.

"Holy shit!" Alan said.

They watched as more black smoke roiled up into the night sky.

"That's pretty awful," Natalie said.

Brandon turned to Rodney, offered him the cigarette.

Rodney realized it was a joint and he said, "Thanks," as he took it, inhaled some smoke.

"Pass it around," Brandon said.

Rodney handed the joint to Heidi, who took a hit, then passed it to Natalie.

"I got a few beers in the car, if anybody wants one," Alan said.

Brandon said, "I got a bottle of whiskey in my car, if anybody's interested."

"I'd like a beer," Heidi said.

Alan drew on the joint, then handed it back to Brandon and went to his car to get the beer.

"I'll take some of that whiskey," Natalie said.

Brandon took another hit off the joint and handed it to Rodney again, then turned and went around his car to the trunk. He opened it and took out a pint of whiskey, then went to the passenger side and opened the door.

"Why don't you come out and watch the fire?" he said.

"I want to go home," Tiffany said.

"Why?"

"Because we shouldn't be here together."

"You just don't want them to see you with me, right?"

She said nothing, just tipped her head back slightly without meeting his eyes.

Brandon studied her face for a moment. She was a lovely girl with short auburn hair and mesmerizing green eyes. She was one of the most popular people at Hope Valley High and she had a reputation to protect; being seen with him was not the way to do that. It was the only thing he disliked about her, that reputation. Because of it, she behaved like some kind of malicious princess.

"Who's out there?" she said.

"Rodney, Natalie, a couple others I don't know. C'mon out."

"They're not my crowd, I'm afraid."

"Yeah, nobody's your crowd except for those plastic mannequin cheerleaders and jocks you hang out with."

"What's burning?" she said.

"BioGenTech."

She sighed heavily. "Why did I come with you? Oh, this is so bad."

"Why? They won't care that you're with me. If you don't come out, they're gonna think you're a stuck-up bitch."

"Did you *tell* them you were with me?"

"No, but I will."

With another sigh, she got out of the car, and the two of them joined the others. Brandon unscrewed the cap on the pint of whiskey and handed the bottle to Natalie. She thanked him and took a couple swallows.

"Pass it around," Brandon said.

"Hi, Tiffany," Natalie said. The others greeted her, as well.

Tiffany said nothing. She stood with her arms crossed over her chest.

They drank beer and whiskey and passed the joint around as they watched the fire grow below them.

"You think it was some kind of bomb?" Natalie said.

Heidi said, "Why would someone want to blow up BioGenTech?"

"Wow, what if it's terrorists?" Alan said.

"That would sure put Hope Valley on the map," Rodney said.

"Hey, look," Alan said. "There's a naked woman on the drive-in screen!"

They all turned to the screen and saw a naked woman being attacked by a man with a knife.

"That's *Thrill Killer,*" Brandon said. "A slasher movie. I saw it a few nights ago."

"Any good?" Alan said.

"Well, there's lots of nudity," Brandon said, smirking again.

The six of them stood around talking as the fire burned below. Tiffany kept a small distance from the others, arms folded tightly across her chest as she stood at the edge of the embankment.

Sirens rose from the town below and they stopped talking to watch the red pulsing lights of two fire trucks race through town down Center Street. That took them through the woods and would lead them to BioGenTech. By that time, the fire had grown considerably.

"They're probably going to need more than two trucks," Rodney said.

Natalie nodded and said, "They'll call in trucks from Newbury and Ridgeton." She took the whiskey from Alan and drank some more, then handed it off to Heidi, who took a swallow.

As they watched the fire, they continued talking about movies and school and what they were doing on spring break, which had started yesterday, Monday.

"I'm doing nothing all week," Alan said. He took Natalie's hand and added, "We've been doing nothing together."

Heidi handed the whiskey to Rodney, and he drank some, then handed it back to Brandon, saying, "What are you doing these days now that you're not going to school?"

Brandon shrugged. "I got a job bagging groceries at Riley's. Sometimes I help my dad at the hardware store." Brandon's father owned Carr's Hardware, the only hardware store in Hope Valley, and often employed teenagers. "Part-time minimum wage teenagers keep money in my pocket," he often said.

They talked about school, teachers and the principal Mrs. Kirtney, who was, unsurprisingly, not very popular with the students.

Time passed as the fire burned below. Arcs of water shot up into the air from firemen's hoses and came down on the flames. Sirens wailed in the night as more firebricks raced to the blaze.

They started kissing, and after a while, Alan said, "We're going back in the car, guys. See you later."

He and Natalie took the rest of the six-pack and got into the back seat of the Beetle.

Brandon walked over to Tiffany and they talked quietly.

Rodney turned to Heidi and smiled, put his arms around her. "Where were we?"

"We were in the car, where it was a little warmer than it is out here. I'm getting kinda chilly."

Rodney turned and said, "Brandon, Tiffany, we'll see you later."

Brandon tossed a wave their way, and Rodney and Heidi got back into the Mustang.

Rodney turned the radio on again. Without speaking, they embraced and kissed. Rodney slid a hand up and cupped her breast, testing the waters. When she did not protest, he slid the hand beneath her shirt. She wore no bra and her nipple was hard as a pebble.

After a while, he lifted her shirt and put his mouth on her breast, and Heidi moaned quietly as she smiled. She slipped a hand between his legs and massaged his erection.

The Mustang's windows clouded up.

Outside the car, at the edge of the embankment, Brandon and Tiffany raised their voices as they spoke. They sounded contentious.

Rodney and Heidi didn't notice.

Rodney felt as if his erection were about to burst through his jeans. Heidi wore jeans, too, and he reached down, slid his hand between her thighs. She pulled her legs apart a little to accommodate him.

A scream rose above the music on the radio, sharp and piercing, then it cut off abruptly.

Five

Rodney and Heidi pulled apart when they heard the scream. The windows were fogged and they couldn't see anything outside.

"Tiffany!" Brandon cried, his voice hoarse, distressed. *"Tiffanyyy!"*

"What the hell is going on?" Rodney said as he opened the door and got out of the car.

Brandon and Tiffany were gone. Rodney thought they'd gotten back into the Toyota until he heard bushes rustling just below the edge of the embankment. He frowned and walked over to the edge.

"Tiffany! *Tiffany!*" Brandon was screaming the name now with great urgency, and he was somewhere down the embankment in the bushes.

"Brandon?" Rodney called. "What're you doing down there?"

Brandon continued to call Tiffany's name. There was a sudden rustle of bushes, then Brandon yelped in pain and said, "Shit!"

"Brandon?"

In the dark, Rodney saw a shape climbing back up the embankment. It was Brandon. Rodney offered a hand and said,

"Let me help you." He noticed Brandon's hand was wet as he pulled him up over the edge. "What happened? Where's Tiffany?"

Brandon breathed hard as he limped in a frantic circle for a moment, looking lost. Then he returned to the edge, bent forward, and leaned his hands on his thighs as he looked down the slope.

Rodney looked at his right hand and saw a dark smudge between his thumb and forefinger.

"It carried her off," Brandon said, his voice hoarse. "God, it just, it-it fucking *carried her away*!"

"Is this blood?" Rodney said, looking at his hand.

"It hurt her, it stabbed her with those, those … they were like these big fangs, these big fucking *fangs*, it closed 'em on her and dragged her down there." Brandon paced back and forth along the edge of the embankment, clenching and unclenching his fists.

Heidi got out of the car and came to Rodney's side. "What's wrong?"

"I'm not sure." Rodney turned to Brandon. "What are you talking about, Brandon? *What* dragged her down there?"

"I don't know, I don't fucking *know*, but it was big, and it had a lot of legs, and it knocked me over with one of them. Her blood spluh … *splattered* on me. Didn't you hear her scream? Didn't you fucking *hear* her?"

The doors opened on the Beetle and Alan and Natalie got out and joined them, straightening their clothes.

"What's going on?" Alan said.

Rodney asked Brandon, "Where is Tiffany now?"

"God dammit, aren't you *listening*?" Brandon shouted. He pointed down the embankment and said, "She's down *there* somewhere! It dragged her down there. I tried to follow but it was too fast. Even though it was carrying her, it was just too fucking *fast*."

"Are you talking about some kind of animal?" Heidi said.

Brandon nodded rapidly. "Yeah, yeah, it was some kind of animal, but it was nothing I ever saw before. It was like—I don't know, it had all these fucking *legs*, and those fang things, they were *huge*."

"Fang things?" Heidi said with a tremble in her voice.

"We gotta get help!" Brandon shouted. "We need guns, we need—*something!*"

"I'll drive down to the sheriff's department and get somebody," Rodney said.

"Not without me, you aren't!" Heidi said.

"What *happened*?" Alan said.

"Some kind of animal dragged Tiffany down the slope," Rodney said.

"No shit?" Alan said. "Is she okay?"

"No, she's not okay, you fucking moron!" Brandon shouted, fists clenched.

"Hey, I'm just asking," Alan said. "I've been busy."

"Come on, Heidi, let's go," Rodney said, taking her hand. "I'll be back with some help."

They got into the Mustang. Rodney started the engine and backed out of his parking spot and headed back down Creasey Hill Road.

Six

The sheriff of Pearce County, Anthony Harker, had been busy in the last hour. He'd been directing deputies to the massive BioGenTech building, half of which was now in flames, and he'd called a few off-duty deputies to come to work and take up the slack. He'd called the Bureau of Alcohol, Tobacco, Firearms, and Explosives and asked that a bomb expert be sent to Hope Valley as soon as possible. Not much happened in Pearce County, and the explosion and fire were big.

Now, he was on the phone with the fire department's arson expert, Hugh Davis.

"When did you say this happened?" Davis said. He sounded groggy.

"About an hour ago," Harker said. "I need you to get out there as soon as you can."

Davis yawned and said, "I'm a pretty early riser, so I was in bed asleep."

"Sorry to wake you, but you're the only arson expert we've got."

"Yeah, I'll get out there right away. But I'm probably not going to be able to tell you anything until they've got the fire down to a—"

"I know, but you can at least question the employees."

"True, true. You going out there?"

"As soon as I can get out of here, I am."

"All right. See you out there."

Harker hung up the phone on his desk, leaned back in his chair, joined his hands behind his head, and sighed. His shift had ended over two hours ago, but as usual, he'd lingered at the station. There wasn't much to go home to—his beagle, Boo, and a TV dinner, maybe a little television if there was anything interesting on.

His wife Trish had left him a little over a year ago, and she had taken their two children—twelve-year-old Peter, and Della, sixteen—with her. They'd been married for eighteen years when she'd left him. She'd claimed he loved his job more than he loved her. While that was not true, he did love his job and it had kept him away from home more than it should have. Two years ago, Trish had taken a computer class at the junior college in Newbury, and she'd ended up having an affair with her instructor. Harker had been surprised by how unsurprised he'd been. But it had hurt. He'd tried to be home more after that, tried to make it work, but Trish's affair had done some damage, and they were unable to recover from it. More accurately, *he* was unable to recover from it. After that, he'd become suspicious of her every time she left the house, every time *he* left the house. No matter how hard he tried to spend more time at home with her and the kids, he found he was unable to look at her without feeling pangs of jealousy and betrayal in his chest. So he'd ended up spending *more* time at work. By the time she'd told him she wanted a divorce, he'd been feeling the same way, so they'd parted rather amicably. She lived in Newbury now, still seeing her college teacher boyfriend. Harker saw the kids every other weekend.

He stood and stretched his arms above his head. He was forty-two, a tall man—six feet, three inches—with a slight paunch. His dark-brown hair was streaked with gray, as was his mustache. He left his office, went out into the station's main room, which contained four desks. It was empty. He was waiting for Deputy Leland Ross to come in. He was late, as usual. As soon as Ross arrived, Harker planned to go out to BioGenTech.

He went into the dispatch room where Anna Huff was just ending a call. Her red hair fell to the top of the chair's back. She wore a sleeveless blouse and he looked at the smooth, pale skin of her arms. She glanced over her shoulder at him and smiled. He waited till she was done with her call, then stepped forward and said, "How's it going?"

"We're still getting calls reporting the fire," she said.

"Anything else?"

"No, besides the fire, it's been pretty quiet."

He bent down and kissed her on the mouth.

She pulled away and smiled. "You know, Leland could walk in any second."

"I wish he would. He's fifteen minutes late as it is."

"Well, we agreed we'd keep this to ourselves, right?"

He nodded. "Yeah, you're right. But I could sure use a little sugar."

"Not at work."

He nodded again.

She reached out and took his hand, pulled it to her mouth, and kissed the back of it.

He smiled down at her. He wanted to undress her, hold her, feel her smooth skin under his hands. They seldom had the chance to be alone together. Anna was married and very cautious. She had no intention of damaging her marriage and had already told him their relationship would go no further than it had already. Harker reminded himself he was doing the same thing Trish's computer instructor had done—having an affair with a married woman. But when he looked at Anna, he found it difficult to care.

They'd made love twice in the back seat of his cruiser like a couple of fumbling teenagers and once in a motel on the outskirts of Ridgeton. It was frustrating, but at the same time exciting. It made him feel young again.

A sound came from the rear of the building and Harker knew Leland Ross had finally arrived.

"See you later," Harker said as he left the dispatch room. He found Ross standing by a desk eating a Slim Jim.

"Do you even *have* a clock that works?" Harker said.

"Sorry," Ross said. "I got a call from a guy who's helping me with research, and I had to take it."

Ross was trying his hand at writing and had been working on a novel called *Cop Killer* for several months. Harker had read some of Ross's writing and didn't think he was going to get anywhere with it, but he kept his opinion to himself. Ross enjoyed it.

"Where is everybody?" Ross said.

"Where the hell have *you* been? There was an explosion at BioGenTech. It's in flames. I need you to hold things down here. I'm going over there."

"No problem."

"Leland, you've really *got* to start showing up on time, or I'm going to have to take some kind of action. Understand?"

The deputy nodded. "Yeah. I will. It won't happen again."

Harker was skeptical.

Seven

Rodney parked in the front lot of the sheriff's department. He and Heidi had put Listerine Breath Strips on their tongues to mask the smell of alcohol. Before getting out of the car, they checked each other's breath.

The night had grown a little cooler and Heidi folded her arms over her chest as they went to the glass door in front of the building.

Inside, there was a row of chairs up against the wall to the left, a drinking fountain in a small alcove on the right. In front of them, a long counter separated the waiting area from a large room with four desks in it. Sheriff Harker stood talking with a deputy between two of the desks.

"Sheriff?" Rodney said.

Harker turned to them, then came over to the counter. "What can I do for you?"

"We need help," Rodney said. "A friend of ours was attacked by some kind of animal and carried off."

"Some kind of animal?" Harker said, squinting a little.

"We didn't actually see it happen," Rodney said, "but another guy did, a guy who was there with her. We were at Lovers' Lookout, and he said some kind of animal came up from the embankment, grabbed her, and carried her down the slope."

"What kind of animal around here carries people off?" Harker said.

"I don't know," Rodney said.

"There was blood," Heidi said.

Rodney held up his hand—a streak of blood was drying on it.

Harker frowned, then sighed. "How long ago?"

"About as long as it took us to drive here from Lovers' Lookout," Rodney said.

"Who's this friend of yours that was allegedly carried away?"

"Tiffany Huff," Rodney said.

The sheriff's eyes widened slightly and he tossed a glance over his shoulder at a window in the wall that looked into another room.

Rodney had forgotten that Tiffany's mother worked dispatch in the sheriff's department.

"Where is she now?" Harker said.

"I don't know," Rodney said. "Brandon went down the embankment a ways, but he couldn't find anything."

"Brandon? Brandon who?"

"Carr."

"Brandon Carr," Harker said, frowning. He nodded and said, "Okay, I'll head up there right away. You want to meet me there?"

"Sure," Rodney said.

Rodney and Heidi left the building and got back in the car. Rodney pulled out of the parking lot and got back on the road.

"Rodney, I don't think there are any animals around here that could carry someone off," Heidi said.

"Yeah, I've been thinking about that, too. Maybe a bear?"

"Possibly. But I think a bear would just attack, you know? They're not too big on carrying people away. Are there any zoos around here?"

"No."

"He said it had a lot of legs."

"Yeah, but what could *that* be? I mean, something with a lot of legs that would carry somebody off like that? It was dark. He couldn't have gotten a very good look at it."

"True."

As he turned onto Creasey Hill Road, Rodney noticed a pair of headlights closing in behind them and assumed it was Sheriff Harker. Halfway up the hill, he pulled into the turnout and parked.

Brandon was still pacing along the edge of the embankment, limping slightly, with Alan and Natalie standing nearby.

Dark smoke still rose from the fire down below.

"Have you seen her?" Rodney said as he and Heidi got out of the Mustang.

"No," Alan said.

The sheriff pulled his cruiser in beside Rodney's car, killed the engine, and got out. "Brandon Carr," he said with a cold smile. He held a flashlight in his right hand. He walked over to Brandon, who stopped pacing. "You want to tell me what happened here tonight?"

Brandon took a deep breath. "I was standing right over there—" He pointed to a spot by the edge of the bank. "—with Tiffany. Then this thing, it came up from the embankment and it was on her, just like that. It knocked her down, and it drove these, I don't know, these, like, *fangs* into her, and it turned around and dragged her back down the embankment."

Harker sniffed a few times. "I do believe that's liquor I smell," he said. "You been drinking?"

Brandon sighed. "A little, yeah."

"Turn around."

"Oh, come *on*."

"Turn around, Brandon."

Brandon turned around and put his wrists together behind his back. He knew the routine.

Harker took handcuffs from his belt, tucked the flashlight under his arm, and put the cuffs on Brandon's wrists. "You're not under arrest, this is just for—"

"My safety and yours," Brandon said. "Yeah, yeah, I know."

Harker casually frisked the boy. "Turn around. Now tell me again what happened, and tell me the truth this time."

"I *told* you the truth."

"What did this animal look like?"

"I don't know, it was dark, I didn't get a good look at it."

"What would you guess it was?"

Brandon sighed and rolled his eyes. "I know how this sounds, but it … it …"

"Come on, let's hear it."

"It had a lot of legs, these big, long legs. Like … like a spider."

Rodney exchanged a look with Heidi. She looked doubtful. Rodney wondered if Brandon had done anything besides the joint he'd been smoking earlier.

Harker stared at Brandon for a while before saying, "A spider. A *spider*. You on something, Brandon?"

"No, I'm telling you—"

"I hear what you're telling me, and I'm telling *you* that if this is some kind of hoax, I'm going to make so much trouble for you, you'll wish you hadn't gotten up this morning, you understand?"

"This is *not* a hoax."

"You're telling me a *spider* carried Tiffany Huff down that bank?"

"I'm telling you it *looked* like a spider."

Harker reached out and touched Brandon's gray shirt. "Is this blood?"

"Yeah. Her blood splattered on me when that thing drove those big spikes into her. It had these four spikes on the front of its head, and all four of them—"

Harker stepped even closer to Brandon and said, "If you've done something to that girl, I'll see you go away for a long time, I don't care *how* old you are, you understand me?"

"I didn't do *anything* to her."

Harker waved Alan and Natalie over. They stood next to Rodney and Heidi. He faced the four of them and said, "I want you to tell me what you saw."

Rodney said, "Well … we didn't see anything. We were in the car, and the, uh, windows were fogged up."

"Yeah," Alan said. "Same here."

"Did you *hear* anything?" Harker asked.

Rodney and Heidi spoke at the same time—he said, "I heard Tiffany scream," and she said, "She screamed."

Alan and Natalie nodded and Alan said, "Yeah, we heard that, too."

"Anything else?" Harker said.

"There was shouting just before that," Heidi said.

"When we got out of the car," Rodney said, "we didn't see either of them. I heard Brandon calling her, and I went to the edge of the bank. He was down there in the bushes, calling for Tiffany."

"So it sounded like they were fighting?" Harker said.

"Not *fighting,*" Rodney said, "but it sounded … you know, like a disagreement."

"When was the last time any of you saw Tiffany Huff?" Harker asked.

They all agreed they'd seen her just before they'd gotten back into their cars.

Harker turned to Brandon. "Didn't I tell you I'd better not have any more trouble with you, Brandon?"

"We weren't fighting," Brandon said. "We were just talking, and it kind of got ... heated, is all. Then that thing came up and—"

"I don't want to hear any more about some animal carrying her off," Harker said. "You come clean with me right now. Where is she?"

"I don't *know*!" Brandon shouted.

"Okay, come have a seat in the car," Harker said. He put a hand on Brandon's shoulder and led him to the cruiser, opened up the back door. Brandon sat on the seat in back, legs still outside the car.

Harker got in the front seat and got on the radio, spoke quietly.

"What the hell's going on?" Natalie said.

Rodney said, "I don't think the sheriff believes Brandon's story."

"What do you think happened to her?" Heidi said.

But no one answered.

Eight

Harker called out two deputies to give him a hand in the search, and in half an hour, he was searching the embankment with deputies Kramer and Hanscom. The beams of their flashlights passed over manzanita bushes, wild grapevines, clumps of tall weeds, and large rocks protruding from the embankment.

Helping them were the two teenage boys who'd been parked at the lookout--Rodney Lepke and Alan Burgess. The girls waited together in one of the cars.

Brandon Carr was still in handcuffs in the back seat of Harker's cruiser.

A mile away, firemen had made some progress with the BioGenTech fire, but flames still raged.

The boys called Tiffany's name repeatedly but got no response.

Harker's eyes followed his flashlight beam, looking for some sign of the girl, as he struggled to keep his footing on the steep slope. He didn't trust Brandon Carr. The boy had been in trouble before, and Harker had always suspected it was only a matter of time before he did something serious. He had a feeling the boy had done just that. Maybe he'd knocked the girl down the slope, or maybe he'd beaten her until she went over the edge. He'd been drinking, that was obvious, and Harker knew Brandon had a nasty problem with anger. He'd seen the boy fly into a rage more than once. Whatever had happened to Tiffany Huff, he knew Brandon had done it, which is why the boy was still in cuffs in the back seat of the cruiser.

Harker's flashlight beam came across something dark on a rock. He stopped and bent forward to get a better look.

It was blood.

Harker suspected the girl had come down the steep embankment the hard way, and probably had hit her head on the rock. He hoped she wasn't too badly hurt. He didn't know the girl well, but he was, of course, quite fond of her mother. He knew they would probably find her at the foot of the slope.

"Sheriff," Kramer said a couple yards down the slope. "Come here." He was holding his flashlight beam on something.

Harker's feet slipped a little as he made his way down to where Kramer stood. "What?" he said as he approached.

"You need to see this," Kramer said. He did not lift his head when he spoke, just continued to stare at something on the ground.

Harker went to his side, followed the flashlight beam with his eyes, and saw Tiffany Huff looking up at him with her mouth open.

"Oh, Jesus Christ," Harker said with a groan.

Tiffany's severed head rested against a rock, staring up at the night sky with dead eyes. Her face was badly slashed, as if someone had sliced a knife across it a few times.

Rodney joined them, followed by Alan.

Harker put a hand on the boy's arm and tried to turn him around. "Go on back up, Rodney, you don't want to see this."

"Oh, shit," Rodney whispered when he saw the head. He stumbled backward up the slope, tripped, and landed on his ass.

Harker turned to Kramer and said, "Come up with me, we're going to search Brandon's car for the weapon."

"You ... you think Brandon did this?" Rodney said. He got to his feet clumsily.

"I know he did it," Harker said.

"Then the weapon is somewhere around here," Rodney said. "He didn't have a weapon when I saw him come up from the slope, and he didn't have a chance to go back to the car."

Harker sighed. "All right, then, we'll look for it here on the slope. Rodney, you go back up, you and your friend."

"Alan."

"Yeah, Alan. I'm going to want statements from all of you, so can you go from here to the station. I'll call ahead and make sure someone is ready to take your statements, okay?"

Rodney nodded. "Yeah, we can do that."

"Good. And I'm sorry, you shouldn't have seen that."

The boy looked at him with wide eyes, lips parted. "I ... I don't understand why Brandon would ... do something like that."

"Nobody understands that sort of thing, Rodney," Harker said. "Nobody but the sick people who do it. You go on up now. Go down to the station." As Rodney started back up the slope, Harker turned to Kramer again and said, "Start looking for a weapon."

"What do you think he did it with?" Kramer said.

"I have no idea." He looked down at the head again, the face white and bloodless, the bloody neck ragged and torn. "It wasn't an easy job, whatever tool he used."

"Where do you suppose the body is?" Kramer said.

"It might have rolled all the way down to the bottom of the slope." He clenched his teeth and shook his head. "That sick son of a bitch. I'm going to have to tell Anna about this." He took in a deep breath and let it out in a loud sigh. "Okay, let's find that weapon."

They searched the slope for the weapon. Twenty minutes passed.

Harker found lots of fast-food containers and wrappers, an old license plate, a rusted tire iron, and mysteriously, an old battered tea kettle. But he found nothing that could have been used to cut off Tiffany Huff's head.

"Sheriff!" Hanscom called. He was down the slope a good distance, maybe at the bottom.

"Yeah?" Harker shouted.

"Down here. I found her."

Harker looked around and determined he was about halfway down the slope. He slid and stumbled the rest of the way down. A few yards away, Kramer was on his way down the slope, too. Before reaching the bottom, Harker spotted Hanscom's flashlight beam beside a large, shelf-like boulder that stuck out from the embankment. He moved diagonally across the slope, toward Hanscom. Harker and Kramer reached the rock shelf at the same time.

"Jesus, this is bad," Hanscom said, and his voice broke.

Harker went to his side and turned his flashlight on the same spot as Hanscom's.

Tiffany Huff's headless body lay beneath the rock shelf, which stuck out about four feet above the ground. She was badly twisted—the arms and legs, what was left of them, seemed to go in all directions. Her clothes were torn to ribbons. So was she.

"Shitfire," Kramer said. "What'd he use to do this?"

Hanscom said, "Look at that—a lot of the flesh is just … it's gone. What do you suppose he did with it?"

It looked like someone had taken an ax to the body. The tissue from the torso and upper legs was gone, exposing raw bones that had been picked clean. Her abdomen had been opened up and it looked like her insides had been chewed up, eaten. Her ribs had been snapped as if someone had gone at them with a pair of bolt-cutters, their jagged ends stuck up like white spikes. Her left forearm had been severed and lay a couple of feet from the body. A thin silver bracelet sparkled on her wrist.

Hanscom said, "She looks like she's been—" He gulped. "—partially eaten. She looks all chewed up."

"You think he … ate her?" Kramer said. "He's gotta be one sick son of a bitch."

Nausea churned in Harker's stomach as he stared down at the mess, at the bone exposed by all the missing flesh.

"He couldn't have done this," Harker whispered.

"What's that?" Hanscom said.

"Carr. He couldn't have done this," Harker said. "He didn't have time to do all this damage. He'd be covered in blood if he'd done this. And to do this, he would've needed … I don't know … *power* tools."

Then this thing, it came up from the embankment and it was on her, just like that, Brandon had said.

"What could've done this?" Harker said, thinking out loud.

Hanscom shook his head and said, "It would have to be a big animal. A mountain lion or a bear."

"Yeah, something big," Kramer said. "It'd have to be."

Harker stepped back and lowered his light. He looked up at the orange glow from the fire about a mile away, reflected in the dark smoke that hovered over it all in a thick cloud.

It had a lot of legs, these big, long legs, Brandon had said.

Whatever had killed Tiffany Huff, it was still out there. And he had no clue what it was.

Nine

Rodney sat next to Heidi in the uncomfortable brown wooden chairs lined up against the wall in the waiting area with Natalie seated on the other side of her. Alan was seated next to one of the four desks on the other side of the counter, being questioned by Deputy Ross, who had already talked to Natalie. The three of them huddled close and spoke in whispers.

"Good thing Alan had some Binaca in the car," Natalie said.

"I had some Listerine Breath Strips," Rodney said.

"Why do you think Brandon would kill her?" Heidi said.

"I don't know," Rodney said. "I mean, he's always been in trouble, you know? But, jeez … to cut off her head. That's just … sick."

Alan came through the gate in the counter and said to Rodney, "It's your turn."

Rodney got up and went through the gate. As he made his way over to Ross, Sheriff Harker came in from the back door with Brandon, who was no longer wearing handcuffs.

"I want you to go into my office and wait for me, Brandon," Harker said. "Right through that door. Just go in there and sit down." As Brandon went into the office, Harker said to Ross,

"Call Shelly and tell her to drop what she's doing and get in here right now. She lives the closest."

"Okay," Ross said as Rodney sat down beside his desk. Ross picked up the phone and punched in a number.

As Ross made his call, Rodney watched the sheriff go to another desk, pick up the receiver, and punch in a number. "Hello, Mark, this is Tony. Look, I need you to get down here right away, can you do that?" He rubbed the back of his neck with his free hand. "No, Anna's fine, but I need you to get down here now. We'll talk when you get here, okay? See you in a few."

Ross finished his call and turned to Rodney. "Okay, I need your name and address."

As Rodney gave Ross the information, the sheriff went into the dispatch room. He pulled a chair over beside Mrs. Huff. He said something, and she took off her headset, put it on the counter. He took her hand, leaned close, and spoke to her very softly.

"*What*?" Mrs. Huff said, her voice high and quavering.

Harker said something else, and Mrs. Huff screamed. He took her in his arms as she began to sob.

Rodney answered the questions asked of him and told Ross what he'd heard and seen at Lovers' Lookout. As he spoke, his stomach turned over inside him. The memory of Tiffany's severed head lying on the ground was brutally vivid in his mind.

A few minutes later, Mr. Huff came in through the front entrance. Harker called him into the dispatch room. Mr. Huff was immediately concerned when he saw his wife crying. Harker said something to him.

"No," Mr. Huff said loudly. "No, that can't *be*." Mrs. Huff stood and leaned against him heavily. He put his arms around her and they both sobbed.

A tall, slender woman came in through the back door. Harker went to her, said something quietly, then they went into the dispatch room together. Harker led the Huffs out of the room and through another open door, into a room with a round table in the center and vending machines against the wall.

The slender woman in the dispatch room seated herself at the console and put on a headset.

Harker went into his office, sat down at his desk, and started talking to Brandon.

When Rodney was done, he left Ross's desk and went back out to the waiting area, where he told Heidi, "Your turn."

He dropped heavily into the chair, leaned forward, put his elbows on his thighs and his face in his hands. He felt as if he were in a dream, as if he would wake up any minute and find himself in his bed.

As Rodney sat up straight again, Sheriff Harker left his office and came out into the waiting area.

"It appears that Brandon Carr did not kill Tiffany Huff," he said quietly. "We found her body, and what was done to it could not have been done by Brandon. It seems there's some kind of dangerous animal running loose. What I want from you is your assurance that you'll stay away from Lovers' Lookout for a while, all right? Can you do that for me?"

They all nodded and agreed.

Harker said, "Now, if you see anything at all out of the ordinary, and *especially* if you see an animal that looks dangerous or rabid, I want you to report it. Will you do that?"

They agreed again.

"Okay. You drive safely tonight." He turned and went back through the gate, back to his office.

Once again, they huddled and whispered.

"An animal?" Natalie said. "What kind of animal takes somebody's head off?"

"Maybe it's a bear, or something," Alan said.

Rodney said nothing. He felt too sick and shaky to speak.

When Heidi returned, they all left.

As Rodney and Heidi walked to the Mustang, he told her what Sheriff Harker had said.

She took his hand. "You're shaking," she said.

"I don't feel so good," Rodney said.

"I can drive, if you'd like."

"You wouldn't mind?"

"Are you kidding? I love your car."

One corner of Rodney's mouth turned up in a half-smile. "My dad gave it to me for my sixteenth birthday. He's a mechanic and owns the garage in Hope Valley. He bought the Mustang a couple years ago for next to nothing. It was on its last legs, and he fixed it up for me, rebuilt the engine, everything. I'm pretty proud of it."

"You should be. Let me drive to my place."

"Okay," he said. He reached into his pocket, fished out the keys, and handed them to her.

Ten

"So you believe me now," Brandon said.

Harker nodded. "I believe you." He took a pen from a holder on the desk and poised it over a yellow legal pad, ready to write.

"Then why am I still here?"

"Because I need you to tell me what you saw. I need you to describe in as much detail as possible what it was that carried Tiffany down that slope."

"I told you already. It was big, it had a lot of legs, hairy legs, and it had these big fucking … um, well I don't know what else to call them besides fangs."

Harker wrote on the pad. "Fangs."

"Yeah. They were black. And there was hair all around them."

"Black fangs." He looked at Brandon, frowning. He had hoped the boy would change his story to something more believable.

"Four of them. Two on top, two on the bottom."

"How tall was it?"

"It was low, maybe three feet tall, no more. But it was broad."

"You say it had a lot of legs. How many, you think?"

"Eight? Ten? And they were long, maybe five feet or so."

Harker's frown deepened. Brandon's story was only getting worse. "What about its body?"

"It was long."

"A long body with eight or ten legs and big black fangs." Harker sighed. He closed his eyes a moment, and in the darkness behind his eyelids, he saw the twisted, torn, headless body of Tiffany Huff. "It sounds like a spider."

"That's what I tried to tell you."

"Brandon, you know as well as I do there's no spider that big."

"If you'd told me that this afternoon, I'd agree with you, but I know what I saw."

"Okay. Okay."

"How am I supposed to get home? My car's still up on Lovers' Lookout."

"I'm going to call your dad. I don't want you driving while under the influence. You can get your car tomorrow. I *should* impound it because you've been drinking, but I'll let it slide this time."

Brandon sighed.

"Is there anything else you can tell me? Anything at all?"

"Yeah. It moved fast. Whatever it was, it was like lightning. It was there, on her, and gone. Like *that*," Brandon said as he snapped his fingers.

Harker nodded as he wrote.

He had no idea how he was going to handle this. He could not warn people about something unless he knew what it was, and he knew it wasn't a spider. How *could* it be?

He remembered that there had been a carnival in Newbury over the past weekend. He wondered if some kind of exotic animal could have escaped from captivity. Was it possible the carnival troupe would pack up and leave without reporting a missing animal? It seemed unlikely, but it was worth checking into.

"Okay, Brandon, I'm going to call your dad. You just sit tight."

Eleven

Heidi lived in Wooded Acres, an affluent development that was only three years old. The two-story houses were large and not very close together. To get there, they had to go through the woods that spread out at the bottom of Creasey Hill.

As Heidi drove away from the sheriff's department, they said nothing for a while. She was the first to speak. "Mind if I turn on the radio?"

"Sure, go ahead," Rodney said.

She turned it on, but neither of them paid any attention to it. The music and voices served as a soothing white noise.

"This evening didn't go very well," Rodney said. "I'm sorry."

"It wasn't your fault. I'm sorry you had to see that."

"I've known Tiffany almost my whole life," Rodney said. "Ever since first grade. I've never liked her much, to be honest, but still ... I can't get it out of my mind, her head lying there on the ground."

Heidi reached over and squeezed his thigh. "That's awful."

She drove down Cutter Way, with dark woods on each side of the road. The Mustang's headlights sliced through the black night ahead of them.

The Nora Jones song ended and a news update came on. A female newscaster reported that the BioGenTech fire was under control, but still burning. Then:

"A teenager was brutally killed in Hope Valley tonight," the newscaster said. "Seventeen-year-old Tiffany Louise Huff was attacked and decapitated at Lovers' Lookout earlier tonight. Sheriff Tony Harker is giving few details, but says he believes the girl was attacked by an unidentified animal."

"An unidentified animal," Rodney muttered.

"What do you think it is?"

"I have no idea." He said nothing for a while. "A bear, maybe? Something strong."

"Do you have bears around here?" Heidi asked.

"Not that I've ever known about."

The news switched to sports, and after that, a U2 song played.

Finally, Rodney said, "How would you like to go to a movie tomorrow night?"

"Sure. What do you want to see?"

"Well, we could go to the drive-in and see *Thrill Killer*."

"A scary movie? After all this? I don't know."

He smiled. "We don't have to watch the movie, you know."

"True. Okay, sounds good."

"We should get something to eat, too."

Heidi said, "We could get a pizza and take it to the movie with us."

"That's a good—"

Something appeared in front of the car. It was a blur that shot out into the road from the woods on the right.

Heidi screamed as she slammed on the breaks.

Rodney was thrown forward against his seatbelt. The Mustang swerved and the tires screamed until the car came to a stop at an angle across the two-lane road.

It had been little more than a golden blur in the glow of the headlights, and then it was gone. It occurred to Rodney, as his heart thundered in his throat, that it was the color of urine.

"What was that?" Heidi said, her words running together. She clutched the steering wheel with white-knuckled hands and her right leg was straight, knee locked, as she continued to press on the brake pedal.

"I don't know," Rodney said, voice hoarse.

"Did you *see* that, did you see how *fast* it was, how *big* it was?"

"Calm down, Heidi."

Her breasts rose and fell with her rapid breaths.

Something slammed into the rear of the car and made it shake.

Heidi screamed again.

Metal crunched in the back and Rodney turned, looked out the back window. Something moved in the red glow of the taillights. It cast a quick shadow on the pavement.

Then it was gone.

"Let's go, Heidi," Rodney said tremulously.

She sat there clutching the steering wheel, her wide eyes staring straight ahead, mouth open, foot still pressing down hard on the brake pedal.

Rodney feared she was in shock.

"Heidi, come on, let's—"

Something slammed into the door on Rodney's side and made the car rock. He cried out in surprise. There was as much fear as surprise in his cry. He turned and looked out the window on his right but saw only darkness.

Whatever it was, it banged into the door again, jolting the car, and this time, a long, sharply-pointed black spike pierced the door. Its point came within a fraction of an inch of Rodney's thigh, and he threw himself to the left.

"Heidi, let's get out of here!" he shouted as he looked at the spike.

The spike pried back and forth, then was ripped out with an abrupt groan of metal.

Rodney moved close to the door again and put his face to the window in time to see only a flash of movement.

"Go, Heidi, *go*!"

She did not move. Her bulging eyes did not blink.

"Heidi*!*"

Something heavy jumped onto the rear of the car, which sunk beneath its weight. The car rocked and bounced with a terrible clattering sound.

Rodney looked back and saw that something crawl over the back window on its way to the car's roof.

"God dammit, Heidi, *go*!"

She made a whimpering sound that was almost inaudible because of the clatter.

A black spike ripped through the vinyl top, followed by two more. They closed together and tore a hole in the roof of the car.

Rodney unfastened his seatbelt, reached over, and pushed Heidi up against the door. He lifted his leg over the gearshift and slammed his foot down on the gas pedal. The engine revved, but the car did not move because Heidi was still pressing on the brake. He reached over and hooked his arm beneath her thigh, pulled her leg up with effort until her foot came up off the brake pedal. The car shot forward and Rodney grabbed the wheel with his left hand to keep it on the road.

"Heidi, let go of the wheel, dammit!" he shouted.

"What's happening what's *happening*?" she cried as she dropped her hands from the wheel, then lifted them to her face.

The black spikes ripped the car's vinyl top further, until a larger hole had opened up.

The Mustang convertible sped down Cutter Way straddling the broken white line down the center of the road.

Rodney reached over and held the wheel with both hands, then pounded his foot down on the brake pedal.

The car screeched to a stop and the thing on the roof tumbled down the windshield and over the hood. It fell to the road in front of the car.

Rodney stared at the thing lying on the road in the car's headlight beams. He squinted at it, then opened his eyes wide, certain they were playing a trick on him.

A cluster of long, hairy, stick-like legs desperately pumped up and down. Rodney realized it was upside down, on its back, fighting to right itself again. It was golden in color, its body long and in two segments. It occurred to Rodney that the thing's body was as long as the love seat in his living room at home, except the love seat, of course, did not have all those legs.

After rocking back and forth and fighting for purchase, it righted itself.

Heidi screamed.

Rodney dragged in a long, rumbling gasp.

It was a spider, just as Brandon had said, an enormous golden spider with legs about five feet long and a black-striped abdomen.

Heidi screamed again and kept on screaming as the creature turned and faced them head-on, then climbed up onto the hood with its back half hanging off. Two black beady eyes positioned very close together stared in through the windshield above the nightmarish maw. Its three black fangs, one on top and two beneath them, articulated separately at the bottom center of its round, hairy face. Rodney realized in a fleeting way that it was missing a fang, the one on the top left side.

He stomped his foot onto the gas pedal and the car bolted forward. He turned the wheel back and forth, swerving the car to the right, to the left, back to the right again.

The spider slid off the hood on the left side and fell to the road, and Rodney got the car on a straight course again, but he did not slow down.

Heidi continued to scream.

Rodney looked in the rearview mirror.

It was following them, *chasing* them. And although it was several yards behind, it was keeping pace with them.

"Stop, Heidi, *stop*!" he shouted.

She stopped screaming and sobbed instead.

He drove faster as he kept glancing in the mirror.

The spider was falling behind.

He rounded a corner with a faint squeal of tires, then sped down another straight stretch.

It was gone. It had given up.

"Did you see that, did you *see* it?" Heidi cried.

"I saw it, all right," he said as he kept driving.

A furniture store commercial played on the radio, completely ignored.

Rodney finally slowed the car to a stop at the side of the road. He put the gearshift in park and unfastened his seatbelt. "We're trading seats, Heidi. Come over here." He pulled on the door handle, but the door stuck. He slammed his weight against it a couple of times and it popped open. He got out and walked around the front of the car to the driver's side as Heidi unfastened her seatbelt, then clumsily climbed over into the passenger's seat as she continued to cry.

Rodney turned to her and put his arm across her shoulders. "Are you all right?"

She was calmer now, sniffling. She nodded erratically. "I-I'm j-just a little shuh-shook up, is all."

"That makes two of us."

Rodney's heart was speeding in his chest, and his hands trembled. He leaned over and kissed Heidi. "You gonna be okay, now?"

"I … I don't know. I mean, I-I-I can't believe we just … *saw* that."

"Neither can I. But that's what Brandon said, remember? He said it had a lot of legs, just like a spider."

She nodded.

"Seatbelts," Rodney said.

They fastened their belts, then Rodney put the car in gear. He checked for traffic, then made a U-turn on Cutter Way.

"What are you doing?" Heidi said, her voice rising higher with each word.

"We have to go back."

"Why? Can't you just take me home?"

"I will if you want, but we've got to tell the sheriff, and he's more likely to believe both of us than just me."

He drove back the way they'd come.

"What if it's still there?"

Rodney increased his speed. "Then I'll run over it."

"We're going back to the sheriff's office?"

"Not right away. There's someone we need to talk to first, someone who can tell us exactly what that thing was."

"Who?"

"My little brother."

Twelve

The crescent moon was an amorphous glow behind the dark smoke from the BioGenTech fire as Rodney drove home. The smoke moved in a thin mist through town, creating halos around the streetlights. The night had grown chillier in the last hour. Rodney drove down Center Street to the southern end of town, where the Lepkes lived in a subdivision called Hope Valley Heights.

Rodney looked at his watch; it was ten minutes after eleven. His parents would be in bed already, which was fine. His dad was going to be very upset about the damage done to the Mustang and Rodney did not look forward to explaining it to him.

His little brother Harold would still be awake in his room, playing a video game or watching a DVD, maybe playing with Gideon, his tarantula.

Rodney pulled into the driveway. Dad's SUV and Mom's Toyota were parked in the closed garage.

"So, you think your little brother will know what kind of spider it is?" Heidi asked as they got out of the car.

"He's nuts for arachnids," he said. "He's got a tarantula, a scorpion. Harry's real smart, but he's a little weird. Kind of a geek."

Rodney went to the rear of the car to inspect the damage.

There was a hole a few inches around in the edge of the trunk. There were two, actually, but one had something lodged in it … something long and black with a lump of viscous pus-like goo on the top end of it. Rodney wrapped his hand around the black object and pried it from the hole in the trunk.

It was about a foot long, as smooth and hard as bone. It was round and cylindrical at the top, but in the last few inches, it became flat and narrow with a serrated edge that culminated in a very sharp tip.

"What's that?" Heidi said.

"When it was in front of the car, I noticed it looked funny that it had only one fang on top," Rodney said. "It lost one in the trunk."

"That's one of its *fangs*?"

"Yeah. My little brother's gonna love this. If he believes it."

Holding the fang in his right hand, Rodney led Heidi up the front walk to the door. His keys jangled as he unlocked the door and they went inside. They went down the hall to the first door on the left, and Rodney knocked quietly.

"Harry?" he said just above a whisper. He didn't want to disturb his parents. He could hear a movie playing in the bedroom. Without waiting for a response, he opened the door and led Heidi inside.

Eleven-year-old Harry sat at his cluttered desk facing the computer screen. He was watching an old black-and-white movie on the monitor. Rodney recognized it as one of Harry's favorites, *Black Scorpion,* about a giant scorpion. Harry must have seen the movie a hundred times, but he never tired of it.

Harry turned in his chair. He'd inherited their mom's blond hair and wore black-rimmed glasses with thick lenses. He was chubby from spending so much time inside and too little time exercising.

There were posters on the walls of spiders and scorpions, including two movie posters—*Black Scorpion* and *Tarantula.* Models of a variety of arachnids covered the shelves on the walls. Hanging from the ceiling in one corner of the room was a spider mobile. Shelves held rows of books on one wall. There were a few regular toys here and there, but the room was dominated by arachnids.

"Hey, Harry," Rodney said.

"Hey," the boy said.

"This is Heidi," Rodney said. "I've told you about her."

Harry stood, facing them. "Hello, Heidi," he said.

"Hi, Harry," she said. "It's nice to—" She gasped.

Harry wore blue pajamas and clinging to the front of the shirt over his chest was a large tarantula.

Heidi stepped back and moved behind Rodney.

"Can you put Gideon away for now?" Rodney said.

Harry went to a shelf that held two terrariums. He gently plucked the tarantula from his shirt, lifted the top on one of the terrariums, and put the spider inside.

"What do you want?" Harry said.

"Harry, you're not going to believe this," Rodney said, speaking quietly.

"Believe what?"

"We just saw a spider."

"So?"

"It wasn't an ordinary spider. It was half the size of my car."

A frown slowly grew on Harry's forehead. "This a joke?"

"No, it's not a joke."

"It's not," Heidi said. "My heart's still pounding from it."

"It attacked my car," Rodney said. "I can show you the holes. You think I'd damage my Mustang for a joke? It also killed Tiffany Huff tonight. And it left this stuck in the hole when it bit the trunk of the car." Rodney held out the black fang.

"Have you been doing drugs?" Harry said as he walked over to Rodney. He took the fang in hand but didn't take his eyes from Rodney's for a moment. "There are no spiders that big."

"Well, there is now, Harry," Rodney said. "Take a look at that thing."

Harry inspected the fang, then looked suspiciously at Rodney. "Did you buy this at the novelty shop over in Ridgeton?"

"No, dammit, I'm telling you, it was stuck in the trunk of my car. The spider actually *bit* the back end of my car."

"What do you want me to do about it?" Harry said, looking at the fang again.

"I want to know what kind of spider it is, then I'm going to tell the sheriff about it."

"The sheriff?"

"It's a long story, Harry, just trust me on this, okay? We're kind of in a hurry."

Still frowning suspiciously, Harry nodded slightly. "Okay. What'd it look like?"

"It's gold colored, and it has a lot of hair on it. Its abdomen has black stripes. And it's got a lot of legs."

"If it's a spider," Harry said, "it's got eight legs."

"Well, it looked like it had a lot of them."

"Can you draw it?" Harry said

"You know I can't draw very well, Harry."

"You can't describe it very well, either."

"Okay, I'll try."

Harry handed the fang to Heidi, then turned to his desk and opened a drawer. He took out a sketchpad, took a pen from the desktop, and handed them over to Rodney.

Rodney took the pad and pen and sat down on the edge of Harry's unmade bed.

As Rodney tried to draw the spider he and Heidi had seen, Harry turned to Heidi and said, "You wanna see my scorpion, Caesar?"

"Uh … not really, Harry," she said. "I'm not too big on bugs."

"Scorpions aren't really bugs," Harry said. "They're 'nids."

"'Nids?"

"Yeah, 'nids. That's short for arachnids."

"Oh. Well, that's nice."

"He's in that tank right over there," Harry said, pointing to the terrarium.

Rodney lifted his head and said, "Leave her alone about the scorpion, Harry, she doesn't want to see it. We've seen enough 'nid for one night."

Harry went over to the bed and sat down beside Rodney, looked at his drawing.

"It had a long, narrow body," Rodney said. "Longer than any other spider I've seen, almost more like an ant. And like I said, it had a lot of legs. More than eight, I think."

Harry studied the picture—the striped abdomen, the stick legs, the four big black fangs in the mouth. Harry stood and went to one of the shelves of books. He removed a large hardcover, sat on the bed again, and paged through it. It was filled with pictures of arachnids, and he seemed to be looking for one in particular.

Heidi sat down on the other side of Rodney.

The boy found the picture he was looking for. It was a color photo that took up an entire page.

"That's it!" Rodney said.

"Yes, that's it exactly," Heidi said. "What is it?"

"It's a sun spider," Harry said. "It's also known as the wind spider, because it moves like the wind. It's *very* fast. But it's not really a spider."

"What do you mean, it's not really a spider?"

"It's a 'nid, but it's not a true spider, 'cause it's got ten legs."

"Well, it may not be a spider," Rodney said, "but that doesn't make it any less dangerous."

"Where is it?" Harry said. "I'd like to see it."

"You don't want to," Heidi said with a small shudder.

"You don't want to go anywhere *near* this thing, Harry," Rodney said. "It attacked my car. It tore a big hole in the roof, a couple holes in the trunk. This thing is vicious."

"If it's a sun spider, it would be," Harry said. "They're very aggressive. They don't just kill for food, they kill for sport. And they have a mouth like—remember the movie *Predator*?"

Rodney and Heidi nodded.

"Well, the sun spider has a mouth kinda like the monster in that movie," Harry said.

Rodney's eyes widened a little. "Yeah, you're right, it did have a mouth like that."

Harry took the fang from Heidi and held it up. "It has four fangs, and each one moves independently. It holds its prey with its front legs while the fangs shred it to bits."

Rodney turned to Heidi. "That's what it did to Tiffany Huff."

"She's really dead?" Harry said.

Rodney nodded and said, "At Lovers' Lookout. I saw her—" Rodney took a deep breath and let it out through puffed-up cheeks. "I saw her head. On the ground."

"It cut off her head?" Harry said with wide little-boy eyes. "You're ... you're serious about this, aren't you?"

"Why would I make this shit up, you dork?" Rodney said. "Is this sun spider venomous?"

"No, it doesn't have any venom. But it'll bite your finger to the bone. And it'll do it for no reason other than to bite you. It's as mean and vicious as it looks."

Rodney took the fang back, handed the sketchpad and pen to Harry, then stood. Heidi stood with him.

"Can we take that book?" Rodney said. "Mark the page, I want to show the sheriff."

Harry turned the pages. "There are pictures of the sun spider's face here, too. Close-ups." He tore the page Rodney had drawn on from the sketchpad and used it as a bookmark, closed the book, and handed it to Heidi.

"Thanks, Harry," Rodney said. "We've gotta go."

Harry stood and said, "Dad's gonna kill you when he sees the Mustang."

"Yeah, I know. Don't tell him, okay?"

Harry nodded as Rodney and Heidi left the room.

Thirteen

Harker held the black spike in his left hand and looked at it closely. He touched a fingertip to the serrated edge. It was like the blade of a steak knife. He looked at the picture of the spider in the open book on his desk, then turned the page and looked at the two close-ups of its face. It was a nightmarish image, like something out of a horror movie. He looked at the fang again, then at the fangs that protruded from the spider's face in the picture.

"You say this is a … a fang?" Harker said.

He sat at his desk in his office. Rodney and Heidi sat on the other side of the desk facing him.

"Yes," Rodney said. "It was stuck in the trunk of my car. It *attacked* the car, Sheriff."

"And you saw it clearly," Harker said.

They both nodded and Rodney said, "It was right in front of the car, in the headlights."

Harker looked at the fang again, at the clump of pale, viscous tissue on the round end. He looked out the open door of his office at the group of about eight reporters and cameramen standing in the waiting area in front. They were waiting to ask him questions about the BioGenTech explosion and fire, and about the death of Tiffany Huff.

He said, "And you just *happened* to have this book handy?"

"It's my little brother's," Rodney said. "He's a spider geek. Well, a 'nid geek."

"A '*nid* geek?"

"Arachnids, 'nids for short. He loves 'nids."

He looked down at the black spike, then at Rodney again and said, "Do you have any idea what would happen if I told my deputies to be on the lookout for a giant spider? You see those reporters out there? They'd eat me alive. I'd be a laughingstock."

"Not if there's really a giant spider out there, you wouldn't," Rodney said.

"And there *is*, Sheriff," Heidi said. "Why would we come to you with this if it weren't true? What could we get out of a hoax like this?"

She was right. They seemed like smart enough kids, and they had to know they'd be in big trouble if they tried to pull a prank on the sheriff's department. As crazy as the story sounded, it made a little sense—Brandon Carr *had* said the creature that carried Tiffany Huff away had a lot of long legs, like a spider.

But how could it be possible? Where would a giant spider *come* from?

"You can come outside and see the damage it did to my car," Rodney said.

"You know what?" Harker said. "I'd like to do that." He opened a drawer in his desk and put the black fang into it, closed the drawer, then stood. "Let's go."

He led them out of his office. The reporters started shouting questions as soon as they saw him heading their way. He smiled at them as he approached the gate in the counter.

"Ladies and gentlemen," he said, "I have to step outside for just a minute, and I promise I'll answer all your questions to the best of my ability as soon as I come back in, okay? Will you wait here for me for just a couple of minutes?"

They agreed as Harker led Rodney and Heidi outside to the front parking lot.

Rodney moved ahead of Harker and led him to the white convertible Mustang parked beneath one of the two sodium vapor lights that illuminated the parking lot.

"See these two holes in the trunk?" Rodney said. "I pulled that fang from this hole. Then the spider came around here."

Harker followed him around to the right side of the car. He looked at the hole in the door.

"Then it got on top of the car and tore a big hole in the vinyl top," Rodney said. "Believe me, Sheriff, there's no way I'd damage my own car to pull some kind of hoax on you."

Harker reached across the roof of the car to the hole in the center.

"Where did you say this happened?" he asked.

"On Cutter Way," Rodney said. "I was taking Heidi home."

He hunkered down and stared at the hole in the door for a long moment, then stuck a finger into it. Frowning, he stood and said, "Let's go back inside. I've got reporters to talk to."

Rodney and Heidi followed.

The second Harker stepped back in the door, the reporters started asking their questions. He held up his hands in a calming gesture as he made his way through the group of reporters and cameramen and went through the gate, behind the counter. He turned to Rodney and Heidi and said, "Go on back to my office and I'll be with you in a minute or two." He turned to the reporters and said, "Now, if you'll just ask one at a time, I'll take your questions." He pointed to one of the reporters and said, "Yes?"

"Sheriff, do you have any idea yet what caused the explosion at BioGenTech?"

"We don't know yet. We've got an arson investigator working on it, we're trying to contact the BioGenTech people, and the BATF in Eureka is sending some people over. As soon as I know what caused the explosion, you'll know." He pointed to another reporter.

"Any idea what kind of animal killed Tiffany Huff?"

"We don't know yet."

"Could it have been a bear? Say, a grizzly bear?"

"It's possible, but not likely. There hasn't been a grizzly bear sighted in this area in about a hundred and fifty years. And so far, we've found no bear prints in the area of the attack."

"What do you *think* it was?"

Would you believe a giant spider? Harker thought as he said, "I don't guess." He pointed again.

"Is it possible that the explosion at BioGenTech could be toxic?"

"I'm not aware of—" He stopped abruptly when two thoughts fell together in his mind.

What if the spider came from BioGenTech? he thought.

"Sheriff?" the reporter said.

"Uh, I'm not aware of … of any …" He was distracted now, preoccupied with the possibility that the bloody mess he'd seen at Lovers' Lookout had been made by something that had come out of the explosion at BioGenTech. "Uh … not that I'm aware of, no."

"Something wrong, Sheriff?" another reporter asked.

"I'm just very busy, that's all. And I'm afraid I can't answer your questions any better than I already have. I've got a lot to do, so I'm going to ask that you clear out of here. As soon as I have some solid information, I'll hold a press conference. Thank you."

They continued to shout questions, but Harker turned and walked away. He went back into his office, where Rodney and

Heidi were seated in front of his desk. He closed the door behind him and dropped heavily into the chair at his desk. When he spoke, he sounded tired.

"You seem like two bright young people. Where does something like a giant spider come from?"

Rodney and Heidi exchanged a look, then Rodney shrugged and said to the sheriff, "One of those old horror movies my little brother watches over and over?"

Harker gave him a small, weary smile.

"From a laboratory?" Heidi said. "Maybe some kind of … mistake?"

Harker nodded, his eyes narrowing slightly. "That was my thought."

"What are you going to do?" Rodney said.

"I'm not sure. This is new territory for me. What I'd like you to do now is go home. Stay inside. Tell your families and friends to stay inside, too."

"Shouldn't you announce this?" Rodney said. "I mean, that thing is out there, and people don't know about it."

Harker sighed. "It might make this my last term as sheriff, but I suppose I'm going to have to do something like that."

"Why do you think it might be your last term?" Heidi asked.

"Telling people there's a giant man-eating spider on the loose isn't exactly the way to win votes. Can I hang on to this book?" He opened the drawer and took out the black fang. "And this?"

"Sure," Rodney said. "The book is my little brother's, but once he finally realizes there really *is* a giant spider running around out there, he'll be so preoccupied, he won't miss it. In fact, he'll be excited that he had some part in it. He'll *love* the idea that you've borrowed his book."

"I'll take good care of it and get it back to you."

"Thanks, Sheriff."

"Thanks for coming in here and telling me all this," Harker said. "You did the right thing."

After they left, Harker sat at his desk and wondered what he was going to do next. He would have to warn his deputies—there were several out at Lovers' Lookout and others at BioGenTech.

He decided to take the book, the fang, and head out to Lovers' Lookout first.

PART TWO

Night of the Sun Spider

Fourteen

Deputy Dixie Cavanaugh slowly passed her flashlight beam over the ground at the foot of the embankment below Lovers' Lookout. Like the other deputies who were scattered around her and above her on the slope, she was looking for tracks that would show a bear or a mountain lion had been through there recently. So far, she'd seen only the tiny tracks of squirrels. Her back ached from bending over for so long and she was getting tired. But until Sheriff Harker said otherwise, they were to keep looking.

Dixie had been off duty watching television with her husband and son when she'd gotten a call from the station to come to work. Otherwise, she would be in bed with her husband Craig now.

She was twenty-nine years old and had short blonde hair. She was plump but curvaceous. She'd never quite been able to lose all the weight she'd gained when she had their son Cory. Craig had not complained; he liked the fact that her breasts were bigger than they used to be, and that made her happy.

She heard rustling in the bushes around her, but assumed it was other deputies.

Her flashlight beam passed over a crushed Coke can as a chilling sound rose from nearby—a man's shrill, ululating scream.

Dixie stood up straight and turned in the direction of the scream.

It went on and on. The sharp crack of a gun being fired reverberated through the night as several frantic voices rose around the scream.

Dixie bolted toward the commotion. She heard others running through the brush and weeds in that direction, too. The beam of her flashlight in her left hand jittered and jumped as she ran. She took her gun from its holster.

The scream was cut off, only to be followed by another cry, a horrified, high-pitched, "No! No! No!"

She darted around manzanita bushes and into a grove of oaks and pines until she saw them—five men, two on the ground, three simply staring in silent shock, their flashlight beams on a creature that Dixie could not understand at first.

Deputy Oliver Hanscom lay on his back on the ground, his arms spread out at his sides. His gun was still clutched in his left hand. The creature that was on him had what looked like a dozen legs, all of which came up from the body, then curved sharply downward. It was yellow in the glow of the flashlights with the back half of its two-segmented body striped with black. It moved on Hanscom and made horrible sounds—slurping, smacking, sucking, and clicking, chattering sounds.

Deputy Charlie Decker was on the ground, too. He tried to crawl away from the creature on Hanscom. Decker seemed to be wounded, and with each movement, he cried out in pain.

The other three—Deputies Herb Lewis, Steve Moody, and Danny Crump—stood as if in shock, their mouths gaping. Lewis and Moody were on her left, Crump on her right with his back against the trunk of a pine tree. Moody and Crump had drawn their weapons, but Lewis was frozen in place, sidearm holstered.

"What're you *waiting* for?" Dixie shouted as she stepped toward the creature. She leveled her gun and fired once, twice.

The creature turned around and faced her, and Dixie felt her mind unravel like a ball of yarn, because it was a spider—a *spider*!—and it looked directly at her.

Moody fired his gun at the creature.

The spider was on him and had him on the ground before Dixie realized it had moved.

Moody screamed as the clicking sounds began. He kicked his legs, flailed his arms, and he fired a round into the air. His scream became a gurgle as the spider made those slurping and sucking sounds. Then Moody fell silent.

Lewis screamed as he turned and ran away. His footsteps faded into the dark.

Dixie wanted to scream, but her throat was dry. She realized she'd been holding her breath. She suddenly sucked air into her lugs, but her breaths came fast as panic set in.

"Help me!" Decker cried in a hoarse, broken voice. "I'm hurt! I think it cut an artery in my leg. I'm bleedin' bad!"

Dixie fired again, and so did Crump.

The spider turned away from Moody, its four fangs spread wide. It was on Crump in a heartbeat; it reared up and pinned him against the tree.

He screamed, "Help me please help me oh god oh Jesus oh—"

His screams were cut off by the clicking, chattering sound. The spider moved almost as if it were humping him. When it backed away, the top half of Crump's body fell forward and landed on the ground. His legs remained standing against the tree.

The spider pounced on Crump's torso and began clicking as it slurped and sucked.

Dixie heard footsteps running toward them from behind. Other deputies probably had come down off the slope when they heard the gunfire.

It all had taken place in the space of ten or fifteen seconds.

Dixie fired her gun at the spider again—two, three, four times.

It turned toward her. The four black, individually articulate fangs, now dripping with blood, were open wide. It moved fast, but for Dixie, it was slow motion. The fangs got bigger as it got closer.

"What's happening?" Deputy Reese said behind her. He cried out when he saw the spider, an inarticulate cry.

The instant it was on her, the spider's fangs began to work. It cut open her abdomen and was eating her organs an instant before she died.

Fifteen

Harker parked in the middle of Creasey Hill Road—there was no room on the turnout with four cruisers parked there already. No one used the dirt road except for teenagers coming to the lookout, so he wasn't worried about getting in the way of any traffic.

Flashlight in his right hand, the spider book tucked under his left arm, he went to the edge of the embankment and looked down, listened. He didn't see anyone, but he heard something. He frowned and cocked his head, trying to identify the sound.

It was someone crying. Someone with a deep voice. A man, maybe. But it was muffled.

"Hello?" he called. "Hello!"

When he got no response, he became suspicious. He unsnapped the strip of leather across the top of his holster, ready to draw his weapon.

The crying continued. He listened carefully, and realized it was coming from behind him. He turned around and faced the four cruisers. He saw a figure at the wheel of one of them, but couldn't tell who it was. He walked over to the car, leaned forward, and looked into the driver's-side window.

"Lewis?" he said when he recognized the deputy. "What's wrong? Lewis?"

Deputy Herb Lewis was blubbering like a little boy who'd just fallen off his bike.

Harker rapped a knuckle on the window a few times, and Lewis yelped and jumped in his seat, cried out, and turned to Harker with wide, teary eyes.

"Roll down the window, Lewis," Harker said.

"You've gotta get outta here!" Lewis cried, his voice high with panic. "Or get in here with me, get in, right now, before it comes!"

"Before *what* comes?"

"It's killing them! It's killing them all!"

"Dammit, Lewis, roll down the window."

"Get in the car! Get in the car for god's sake, Tony, before it comes!"

Sighing with frustration, Harker walked around to the other side of the car and got in, closed the door. "What's going on, Lewis? Tell me."

"It had so many legs, that thing, it was …" He stopped a moment and clenched his eyes shut, shook his head, and spoke through clenched teeth. "It was a spider, Tony. A huge spider. And it killed Hanscom, and hurt Decker, and it was gonna kill 'em all, so I ran, I had to run, my god, I couldn't just stand there and be next, I *couldn't*!"

Oh, shit, Harker thought. "Where did this happen, Herb? Where?"

Lewis nodded toward the edge of the embankment. "Down there. In the woods."

Harker put the spider book on the dashboard, the flashlight on the floorboard, and grabbed the radio microphone. "Dispatch, Harker. I need backup at Lovers' Lookout, *now*. Backup at Lovers' Lookout."

"Ten-four," Shelly said.

Harker replaced the microphone.

"It's a spider, Tony," Lewis said. "A *spider*! How can that *be*?"

"I don't know, Herb. I don't know."

Harker wasn't sure what to do. He wanted to get down there to his deputies, but he was afraid that if he went down alone, he'd end up dead and then be no good to anyone. But it had to be done. He took the shotgun mounted between the seats and opened the door.

Lewis gibbered, "No, Tony, don't go out there, don't, don't, it's huge, and it's *fast*, it's so fast you can't even *see* it move, it's just sort of, sort of *gone*, and then it reappears somewhere *else*."

"Who was down there?" Harker asked.

It took several seconds because he stuttered and stammered, but Lewis listed off the names of the deputies down in the woods with the spider.

"Oh, Jesus," Harker whispered. "Look, Herb, you stay here, okay? Just stay right here in this car, don't get out. I've got more deputies coming. Tell them to bring their shotguns down the slope. You hear me? Will you tell them that?"

Lewis nodded jerkily.

Harker took the flashlight from the floorboard, pushed the door open, and got out.

"It'll kill you all, it will, it'll kill you and then it'll eat you, don't go, don't go down there, *don't fucking go*!"

Harker closed the door and went to the edge of the embankment. He made his way down the slope as fast as he could without falling.

"Cavanaugh!" he called. "Decker! Moody!"

No response.

Every little sound he heard made him jump.

He swept the flashlight back and forth as he zigzagged between the manzanita bushes. He went into the darker part of the woods, among the oaks and pines.

He heard rustling in the weeds behind him. He spun around and it stopped. He started to turn back and heard it again, then again. It was getting closer.

Harker aimed the shotgun low, ready to shoot.

Whatever it was, it wasn't very big. It got closer. He saw a small shape in the weeds.

It meowed at him. It was a calico cat.

Harker sighed with relief, then turned around and continued on.

When he found them, he had to look away for a moment. It was Tiffany Huff all over again, but now there were seven of them. At first, he thought there were eight, then he realized Crump was in two pieces.

"Oh, Jesus holy Christ," he said in a breath as he turned the flashlight on each of them, one after another.

Their uniforms had been shredded, abdomens ripped open, organs eaten. Their thighs were gone, with only femurs left behind, the bones picked clean. Their throats had been ripped out and eaten, heads almost severed on a couple of them.

They stared up at him with dead, dull eyes.

He shone the flashlight all around, but there was no sign of the spider. He was relieved by that. His eyes welled up with tears as he looked over the small massacre again. He clenched his teeth and ground them together a little. Sick to his stomach and feeling weary, he turned around and headed back for the slope.

The coroner would be paying his second visit of the night to Lovers' Lookout.

Sixteen

Harker assembled the other deputies who'd arrived at Lovers' Lookout. They stood behind the four cruisers parked in the lookout.

"I'm going to get on my radio," he said, "and I want you to hear what I have to say. I'm telling you now, this is not a joke. Listen close."

There were three deputies there, and they followed him to his car. Harker got in, and they closed around his open door. He took the radio microphone and depressed the button with his thumb.

"This is Harker to all units," he said. "You're not going to want to believe what I have to tell you. I don't have time to try to convince you, so for the sake of your job, you're just going to *have* to be convinced. If I hear of anyone expressing even a *little* disbelief, I'll shitcan you, understand me? You *have* to believe me, your lives will depend on it. There is a big spider in Hope Valley. I repeat, a *very* big spider. It's a sun spider, and it's got a body about five feet long and ten long legs. This spider is *very dangerous,* and it is *very fast*. Take your shotguns with you wherever you go, and if you see it, empty them into it. Do. Not. Hesitate. I repeat, this is a very dangerous, very fast spider. You see it, shoot to kill. Harker out."

Harker put the microphone back and got out of his car. He turned to the deputies.

"You all get that?"

All three deputies nodded.

"Anybody got a problem with it?"

They all said, "No, sir."

"If you don't believe it now," Harker said, "you'll believe it when you see the corpses down there in the woods. Get the coroner down here and tell him to bring the wagon. And call an ambulance for Lewis. He's lost his fucking mind with fear and needs to be sedated, or something. And move your damned cars so I can get out of here."

Harker waited while the deputies moved their cars. He drove farther up the road where there was a place he could turn around, then headed down the hill.

One question repeated itself over and over in his mind: *How in the hell do you go after a spider?*

He knew of no way to lure or track it. It moved fast, so it could cover a good distance in a short time—who knew where it might turn up again?

Harker wasn't even sure he knew where he was headed.

He thought of the book he'd left on Lewis's dashboard, and considered going back for it. The book might provide some valuable information about the sun spider.

The book reminded him of Rodney Lepke. He'd known enough to get the book. He'd said his little brother was some kind of spider geek. Harker didn't know of spider experts he could consult immediately. And even if he did, he thought he might check with the kid first.

He got on the radio.

"Two-oh-six," he said. He was more collected now and gave his I.D. number instead of using his name. "I need a street address for a Lepke, no first name."

He waited until Shelly gave him the address in Hope Valley Heights. He flicked on his siren and lights and got there as fast as he could. He turned the siren off as he passed through the subdivision. There was no point in waking up everyone in the neighborhood.

Seventeen

It was T.J. Stone's last delivery of the night and he wanted to get it over with. He wanted to go home and take a book to bed and read himself to sleep. He read a lot of science fiction and usually had two or three books going at once. He kept them scattered throughout the apartment so whatever room he happened to be in, he could pick up the nearest book and lose himself in other universes.

It was so much better than delivering pizzas.

T.J. was twenty-three and had two jobs. Some nights, like tonight, he delivered for Prime Pizza in Hope Valley, and other nights, he delivered for China Express in Newbury. On weekends, his friend Stanley paid him to help build Stanley's new house in Ridgeton. When they were finished with the house, T.J. would find some other weekend work. He made enough money to live on and to support his book-buying habit, as long as he bought his books at flea markets and yard sales and used bookstores. Not that he needed to buy more—his apartment was cluttered with stacks of hardcovers and paperbacks he had not yet read. In his bedroom, he'd cut through the stacks of books a narrow path that allowed him to get to his desk and bed.

He rolled down the window; the cool spring air felt good on his face. He cocked his left elbow and propped it on the edge of the open window.

T.J. turned on the radio. It was tuned to the heavy metal station, and an old AC/DC song was playing, "Back in Black". He turned it up until the beat was pounding through the car's body.

He stopped at a red light and waited, moving his head to the beat.

He saw movement from the corner of his left eye and turned to find himself looking into a monstrous face with three enormous black fangs. It closed those fangs on his arm. As T.J. pulled away from the window with a gasp, the face pulled away from the car and disappeared.

T.J. looked down at the bloody stump that jutted from his shoulder. As he screamed, he stiffened his legs and his right foot slipped off the brake and hit the gas. The car lurched forward into the intersection. An oncoming car on the left slammed into T.J.'s front end.

T.J. continued to scream.

His car came to a stop diagonally at the corner of the intersection. He tried to pull the parking brake, but his quaking hand kept missing it. Finally, he gave up and struggled with the seatbelt as he made throaty whimpering sounds. He felt warm blood running down his left side from the stump that used to be his arm. Once he unfastened the seatbelt, he reached over with his right hand and opened the door. He fell out of the car, screaming for help.

Blood continued to pump from the jagged stump of his arm.

Eighteen

Sixteen-year-old Lizzie Turner's shift had begun only an hour ago, and yet she was already thinking about going home. Her parents started drinking around five or six, and they got into a fight almost every night. She was so tired of it that she would offer to do some overtime work for no pay to avoid going home until she knew they were in bed.

She put two Max Burgers and an order of curly fries into the white Max Burger bag, then handed the bag through the window to the woman in the minivan waiting outside.

"You have a good night," Lizzie said.

"Thanks, you too," the woman said as she drove away.

The bell rang—another user had just driven over the cable across the concrete by the menu. They referred to their customers as users because so many of them came back again and again, as if addicted to Max Burgers. Those who came in regularly were called *heavy* users. And *heavy* was exactly what most of them were.

A Chevy pickup truck pulled up to the window. Lizzie made change for the man at the wheel, put together his order, and handed it through the window.

The bell rang again.

"You have a nice night, now," Lizzie said.

The man drove away without comment.

The bell rang repeatedly—ding … ding-ding … ding …

"Are them kids out there messin' with the bell again?" Mandy said as she walked by.

"I'm not sure," Lizzie said. She looked up at the monitor. The outside camera mounted on the brightly lit menu showed no one near the cable.

Lizzie leaned out the order window and looked to her right.

Something big but hunched up came around the corner and headed straight for her, something fast—*frighteningly* fast. It was on Lizzie before she could pull herself through the window, and its fangs closed around her head. With a quick, crunching movement, it took Lizzie's head off. It dropped the head and pressed its face to the spurting stump of her neck and sucked at the blood as Lizzie's body slowly slid backward, then fell to the floor inside Max Burger.

Mandy was the first to see her, and the first to scream.

Nineteen

Monty Burnham went out his back door and flicked on the flashlight in his hand.

Something had knocked over all the garbage cans beside the house. He'd just shut down his computer in the bedroom and had been about to go to bed when he'd heard the terrible clatter. His wife Connie was in the living room watching television.

Monty wore his robe and a pair of corduroy slippers. The night air was chilly on his bare legs. He stepped onto the back lawn and swept the flashlight across the yard.

Something moved just outside the glow of the beam and Monty shifted the flashlight to the right to follow it. The beam landed on the big doghouse he'd made for Tucker, their St. Bernard.

Whatever it was, it had gone into Tucker's house.

Tucker was usually in at this hour, but on that night, Monty's eight-year-old son Chris had talked him into letting Tucker sleep in his room. When he'd finally acquiesced, Monty had told Chris not to get used to it, that it was a one-time thing.

"What is it?" Connie said.

Monty turned around and saw her standing in the back doorway.

"I think there's a dog in Tucker's doghouse," he said as he headed for the doghouse in the back corner of the yard.

Connie turned to go back inside.

"Pretty ballsy dog," Monty said with a chuckle, "walking into another dog's—"

There was an explosion of spindly legs that came out of the square doghouse door, and the legs pulled with them a body. The spider blossomed like a flower from the doghouse, and it was on Monty before he could finish his sentence.

Twenty

"Monty?" Connie said as she turned back toward the yard. There was a note of alarm in her voice because she'd heard Monty make a sound like a *yelp*. She saw the flashlight drop to the ground and Monty went down. She stepped out onto the back porch and said, "Monty, what's *wrong*?"

She heard more than saw something moving toward her. It made a quiet thumping sound on the ground, which grew louder as it neared, and in the dark, all she could make out was a blur of movement.

Connie spun around and went inside. She swung the back door hard behind her as she ran through the kitchen, but she did not hear the door shut. Instead, she heard thumping and scraping on the kitchen floor, following behind her.

She ran down the hall to the closet where Monty kept his rifle. Connie opened it and reached in—

—but something grabbed her from behind and lifted her as it pulled her back away from the open door.

Connie's scream became a strangled cough as the spider's fangs entered her back.

Twenty-One

Jerked from his sleep, Chris Burnham sat up in bed when he heard his mother scream. He found Tucker sitting on his haunches at the door, staring at the knob. Chris swung his legs over the edge of the bed and wondered if he'd really heard that, or if he'd dreamed it.

Tucker got up, walked in a circle, then sat down and stared at the doorknob again with a quiet whine.

Chris stood, went to the door, and opened it.

Tucker hurried out the door and his claws clicked on the hardwood floor as he went up the hall.

Chris scratched the back of his head and yawned. He turned and started to shuffle back to bed in his *Star Wars* footed pajamas when he heard Tucker whine again. The whine started high and went low, then stopped.

He heard what sounded like a distinct *crunch* sound, followed by a dull thump.

Chris went back to the door and stepped out into the hall. "Mom?" he said as he turned his head to the right.

The closet door was wide open, and a few feet away from it lay his mother. Beside her lay Tucker.

"Mommy?" Chris said again, but higher in pitch, as he hurried up the hall to his mother's side.

There was so much blood. She lay face down, and there were three big, bloody holes in her back.

Tucker lay beside her, and a couple of feet from the dog was the dog's head.

Chris's vision blurred with tears as he lifted his eyes to look at the dark, open closet. He sobbed as he wiped away his tears.

The darkness in the closet moved. Long, skinny legs curled out of the open doorway and pulled a golden body out into the hall.

Chris knew he had to be dreaming. How many times had his parents told him there was no such thing as monsters? How many times had they told him they were only in movies, they were only special effects? How many times? And here, right in front of him, was a big, hairy, full-blown monster, as big as life, so he had to be dreaming. Even when he screamed, he knew he had to be dreaming, and he would wake up any second now, open his eyes and sit up in bed, and Tucker would be there, and he'd be able to pet him, and everything would be normal and safe.

But he did not wake up.

The spider moved forward and closed its fangs on the screaming boy.

The house fell silent for a moment. Then the hallway filled with the wet sounds of sloppy sucking and eating.

Twenty-Two

Maxine Pruitt sighed as her fat, sweaty, whiskey-reeking husband rolled off her with a sound like a knife slicing through cold ham.

Harvey flopped onto his back and belched, scratched his belly. He'd be asleep in two minutes.

Dudley—or "Duds," as Harve called him—barked out in the back yard. He was some kind of shepherd mix, a mutt, really, but loveable. He also had an annoying bark.

Maxine lay there with her legs still spread, Harve's mess between them. She usually took a shower afterward. She used to shower and masturbate, but that had become too much work, and seemed rather pointless, really. Besides, she could masturbate anytime—why would she do it after lying beneath Harve for a few smelly minutes?

Harve snored. He sounded like someone was torturing zoo animals. She'd told him several times that he probably had sleep apnea and he should see a doctor about it, but he never listened to her.

Maxine sat up on the edge of the bed, sighed again, then told herself to stop sighing. She stood and put on Harve's old robe, a tent of burgundy velour. She liked the way it engulfed her.

She left the bedroom in bare feet, padded down the dark hall to the bathroom and took a quick shower. She dried off, put the robe back on, and went down the hall to her daughter's room. The soft blue glow of Dana's Harry Potter nightlight fell into the hall. Five-year-old Dana didn't like to sleep with the door closed, so Maxine always left it open at night. She went to her daughter's bedside.

Dana was lying on her side with her back to the door. She made a soft little snoring sound that made Maxine smile.

Dudley still barked out back. She wondered, had he been barking all this time and she'd been too preoccupied to notice? Probably a neighborhood cat. But Dudley seldom barked at anything for long.

She went down the hall to the kitchen. She wanted something to drink but wasn't sure what. Tea? Wine? She didn't drink often—watching Harve get drunk every night had turned her off of liquor, for the most part. But a glass of wine sounded good right about now. It sounded civilized, especially compared to Harve's swilling.

They'd talked about his drinking problem, and it always ended with him saying, "I've got it under control."

She'd seen him shake in the morning. She knew he started early, after she left for work. That was why she took Dana over to her sister's house each day. Barbara had two kids of her own, Tommy and Denise, and the girls were the same age. They enjoyed playing together. Barbara's husband James had a good job with UPS, a job he valued and worked hard to keep.

Harve once had a good job at Merriweather's Feed. That didn't sound like much, but he'd made manager, and the feed store was owned by Ozzie Merriweather, a wealthy old man who believed in taking good care of his employees, providing benefits and retirement plans. It was a coveted job from Hope Valley to Ridgeton, but openings were few. Once you worked for Merriweather, you hung on to that job with all you were worth. The only reason Harve had made manager was that the guy who'd managed him had died, and Harve had been there the longest of the low-level employees. It was a huge feed store that serviced rancher farmers throughout the entire county.

Harve had been caught drinking. He'd been warned. Old man Merriweather himself had a talk with Harve and had offered to get him treatment. Harve had insisted he didn't need it. He'd become so obstinate that the old man had fired him then and there.

Maxine opened the bottle of two-dollar wine she'd bought some weeks ago with the thought that a glass or two now and then would be nice. She poured the white wine into a cheap wineglass from a set they had in the cupboard and never used.

She left the kitchen. It opened on a tiny corner dining area with a small oval table and four chairs. She and Dana still ate meals at the table, but Harve always ate in front of the television. The dining area opened to the living room. She went there, put her wineglass on an end table, and flopped onto the couch. She turned on the TV with the remote and flipped through the channels. She didn't know how much longer they'd be able to afford cable. Harve would be devastated, of course. Maybe he'd get off his ass and do something if he didn't have television to watch.

Dudley was still barking. If he didn't stop soon, she'd go out and tell him to shut up. All she needed to do was piss off one of the neighbors she hardly knew.

Maxine knew she should be sleeping. She worked two jobs—eight hours a day waiting tables at the twenty-four-hour Oven Mitt Café next to the truck stop, then she cleaned several houses over in Wooded Acres once or twice a week.

Harve still clung to the lie that he was looking for work. Half the time, Harve couldn't look for his dick. The rutting she'd endured tonight was rare and getting rarer.

She remembered the early years of their marriage, when he was still slender and muscular, back when they couldn't keep their hands off each other. It seemed a lifetime ago, almost like something she remembered from a book she'd read. It wasn't quite real enough to miss anymore.

Maxine preferred to stay in shape. Even though Harve never noticed, she still looked good. She still jogged whenever she had the chance and still got admiring looks from the bagboys at the grocery store, which made her feel pretty damned good.

Maxine lived for Dana. They'd been married ten years when they'd had Dana, and Maxine had seen the way the wind was blowing then. She'd never given but the most cursory thought to getting out. Maxine and her parents, and Harve and his parents, were all very Catholic. Divorce was not an option. Neither of their parents would approve of a divorce. Harve had stopped going to church with her years ago, something the parents on both sides complained about a lot.

Dudley continued to bark. Maxine decided to ignore it for the moment. She was enjoying her wine.

Twenty-Three

Rodney paced his bedroom with the radio on, tuned to the local news/talk station, as he talked quietly with Heidi on the phone.

"They're talking about space aliens on the radio," Rodney said.

"You're kidding."

"No, really. There's this guy who says he knows a guy in some other country who's been in touch with aliens called Pladians, or something, for years."

She laughed quietly. "Do you believe him?"

Rodney thought about that. "You know, after tonight, after what we saw ... it's hard not to wonder what *else* is out there."

After a long pause, she said, "Yeah, I know what you mean. I had a hard time believing it while I was seeing it."

"Me, too. It's almost as if—"

The doorbell rang.

"Whoa," he said, "somebody's at the door. Hang on." He left his room and hurried down the hall before the bell rang again. He didn't want to disturb his parents. He looked out the peephole. "It's Sheriff Harker, and he's got a shotgun." He opened the door. "Hi, Sheriff."

"Sorry to bother you so late," Harker said.

"No problem. Come in." Rodney stepped aside, the phone still to his ear, then closed the door behind Sheriff Harker.

"I need to talk to your brother."

"My brother?"

"You said he was a … spider geek?"

"Yeah."

"I need to know as much as I can about the sun spider. Can I see him?"

Down the hall, Rodney saw light under Harry's bedroom door. He walked in without knocking and found Harry at his desk watching *Kingdom of the Spiders*.

"Why aren't you asleep?" Rodney said.

"With a giant spider loose? I'm all psyched!"

"Be quiet, I don't wanna wake Mom and Dad. Sheriff Harker's here, he wants to talk to you."

"Sheriff wants to talk ta *me*?" Harry's eyebrows rose above the rims of his glasses.

"Yeah, come on."

Rodney led him back up the hall. Harker had turned on a lamp in the living room and sat on the edge of Dad's club chair, the shotgun across his lap. He stood when they walked in and held the shotgun with the barrel down.

"Harry?" he said. "I need to ask you some questions."

"About the spider?" Harry said with undisguised excitement.

"Yes. About the spider. I need to know how to kill it."

Harry nodded at the shotgun. "That'd prob'ly do it. It's big, but I'm assuming it's not indestructible. A shotgun should kill it."

Harker nodded. "Okay. Then how do I *lure* it?"

Harry looked at Rodney, then at Harker. "I dunno. Far as I know, there's no way to *lure* a sun spider. Sun spiders pretty much go wherever they want and eat whatever they want to eat. They're mean and pissed off."

Harker nodded again, but wearily this time, clearly disappointed and frustrated. "Okay. Okay." He stood. "Anything you can think of that I should know?"

"Don't try to outrun it," Harry said. "Kill it as soon as you see it. It moves so fast, you'll be lucky to get off a shot."

"Thanks, Harry," Sheriff Harker said.

"What the hell's going on?" Dad said.

Rodney turned around and saw his dad standing in the hall in his boxers.

Oh, shit, Rodney thought. He said, "Dad. Uh, the sheriff's here."

"I can see that," Dad said. "What's the problem?"

Harker said, "Sorry to disturb you, sir. I came to talk to your son. He knows a lot about spiders, and right now, I've got a great big spider running around killing people."

"A … spider?" Dad said.

"Your sons will tell you about it," Harker said. "I've gotta go. You folks stay inside at all times. Keep all your windows and doors closed and locked."

"A spider?" Dad said again.

Harker went to the door, then turned back to Dad. "Listen to your sons. They're telling you the truth." He left.

Dad turned to the boys, his mouth open, eyes sleepy. "What's going on? And how did *you* guys get involved."

Rodney took a deep breath. "Come in and sit down, Dad. I'll tell you everything."

Twenty-Four

Maxine dozed a little on the sofa as she watched one of the shopping channels. The jewelry shows were her favorite.

Dudley was still barking.

She rubbed her eyes and got up, went back to the kitchen. She stood at the sliding glass door that led out to the back yard.

Dudley yelped a couple times, then cried out. The dog's cry was cut short.

Maxine stopped breathing a moment and listened. She could see nothing through the glass door with the kitchen light on.

"Dudley?" she whispered.

Her breath trembled as she exhaled. She turned and opened the drawer at the end of the counter. From the mess of candles, matches, rubber bands, paperclips, and pens, she removed a twelve-inch red flashlight. She turned it on and slid the glass door aside.

As she stepped out onto the small concrete patio, she heard ... *something*. She crossed the patio to the grass, which was cold and damp beneath her bare feet, and raised the flashlight. She sent the beam into the back corner of the yard.

Slurping, that was what she heard. Sucking and slurping.

An alarm went off in the back of her mind, and her chest felt tight.

"Dudley?" she said.

Maxine passed the flashlight to the left, across the back fence, and it landed on something that was moving, something big with a lot of legs, and it was on Dudley, who lay still on the grass. It was moving on top of Dudley, this thing, and made those sounds, those horrible slurping and sucking sounds, and—

—it stopped.

Maxine's heart beat so hard, it prodded the backs of her eyeballs. She swallowed a whimper as she backed up, heading for the open sliding door.

It turned around. Big glistening black things moved on its face.

"Oh, shit," Maxine said as she turned and ran through the open door. She spun around, slid it closed, and locked it as something slammed into it hard enough to spread a web of cracks throughout the glass.

She screamed as she threw herself backward and fell on her ass. The thing on the other side of the door watched her. That whimpering sound made its way out of her because the thing had Dudley's blood on it and it had smeared the blood on the glass, and if it hit that glass one more time, it would probably get through. But that wasn't the worst of it. The worst of it was the thing itself, a thing she knew in her mind could not exist, and yet there it was, a spider big enough to crack the glass in her door.

Maxine clambered to her feet and frantically looked around the kitchen for the phone, where was the phone?

"Where the fuck is the *phone*?" she whispered harshly.

The base was on the counter, but the receiver was gone.

She ran into the living room.

The thing outside pounded against the glass door again. Maxine heard the crack, but it hadn't broken open. Not yet.

The phone was on the end table at the other end of the couch. She snatched it up and ran back through the living room, past the small dining area and the glass door—

It was backing up from the door, preparing to ram it again.

—and down the hall to Dana's room, where she turned to close the door—

She heard the glass in the door break and jingle as it fell in.

—and she heard it coming, heard its legs thumping over the floor.

She slammed the bedroom door and locked it. She walked quickly backward away from it until she hit Dana's bed and flopped into a sitting position on the mattress.

Dana sat up and squinted at her. "What's the matter, Mommy?"

"Just lie down, honey, okay? Just lie down and—"

It thumped over the floor and up onto the wall in the hallway, then knocked against the door.

Maxine gasped as her head jerked toward the door. She stared at it a moment, then turned back to Dana and said, "Just get under the blankets and cover your ears, okay? Will you do that for Mommy?"

"But what's—"

"Just *do* it, honey, *please*."

"Okay." She lay back down and pulled the covers up over her head.

The thing outside went back and forth. Its legs thumped unnervingly over the floor and wall and door.

"Keep it together," she said, breathing the words to herself. She looked at the phone, turned it on, punched nine-one-one, and put it to her ear.

Twenty-Five

Harker had driven slowly through Hope Valley Heights, up and down every street, and even down the cul-de-sacs. Cats darted across the streets through the beams of his headlights. A dog had chased him a few yards. If there were still cats and dogs roaming the streets, chances were the sun spider had not been through there. Not yet.

He left the neighborhood behind and went to the next development, where he did the same thing.

Shelly's voice came over the radio. "I got a woman who says she has a spider in the house. Thirteen forty-two Sunset Way, one-three-four-two Sunset Way."

Harker immediately made a U-turn and left the neighborhood. He flipped on his lights and siren.

"I'm on my way," he said. "I'll want backup. Is she still on the line?"

"Yes."

"Tell her to get into a room and close the door, then try to get out a window."

"She's already in a separate room."

"If she can't get out a window, tell her to stay where she is and—"

Twenty-Six

"Don't open that door," the woman on the phone said.

"Hang on," Maxine said, "I'm going to try the window."

She put the phone on Dana's dresser and went to the window on the back wall. She unlocked it and slid it open. There was a screen on the outside. Maxine pounded it with her fists, pushed at the edges, then pounded some more.

Something suddenly changed about the sounds the creature was making in the hall outside the bedroom. It had thumped over the door, but it had not come back—it had kept going down the hall.

Maxine turned to look at the wall between the two bedrooms.

Harve, she thought.

She listened as she stared at the wall.

The bed creaked.

Harvey screamed. It was a high, shrill scream and it abruptly ended in a low gurgle.

Maxine stood with her mouth open, looking at the wall.

Dana sat up, eyes bulging with fear. "Mommy, what's happening?" she said, near tears.

Maxine rushed to her side and picked her up. "C'mere, honey, c'mere." She set her down under the window, then went back to work on the screen. "Just stand right there, honey."

Dana began to cry.

"Please don't cry, Mommy needs you to be strong, okay? Can you be strong for me?"

She heard a siren. She listened a moment—it was getting louder.

"Oh, god, please make them hurry," Maxine whispered, closing her eyes for a moment. She continued pounding at the screen as Dana cried. The top corner came loose, and she worked harder. The bottom corner gave and she bent half the entire screen outward. She turned to pick up Dana to send her out the window, but she stopped and looked at the wall again.

What if the thing in the next room decided to go back outside?

Maxine walked over to the wall and listened.

The siren got louder, closer.

She heard clicking in the other room, and wet sounds. Ugly sounds. She remembered seeing it on Dudley, and she realized now that it had been eating the dog.

That was what it was doing to Harve now—eating him.

Maxine was filled with a terrible shame when she realized all she could feel was relief.

Twenty-Seven

Harker arrived first. He parked at the curb, grabbed the shotgun, and got out of his cruiser. The red and blue lights throbbed over the sidewalk and lawn. He racked the shotgun as he approached the house.

Another cruiser arrived right behind him. He looked back over his shoulder and saw Deputy Walter Barrens get out of his car, shotgun in hand.

"We're over here!" a female called. "Over here!"

Harker followed the voice. It came from the side of the house. He jogged across the unmowed front lawn and around the corner.

The woman peered at him through the bent-open screen.

"There's a key to the front door on top of the porchlight," she said. "It's in one of those magnet thingies. You just slide it open."

"Is the spider still in there?" he said.

"Yes, it's in the next room eating my husband. Down the hall, second door on the left."

Harker was startled by the casual way she said it. But he knew people behaved strangely when in stressful circumstances. He jogged back around the corner to the front door—Barrens was already there—and took the key in its magnetic container off the top of the porch light.

"Is it in there?" Barrens said.

"Yep. Back bedroom." He opened the screen door, used the key to unlock the front door, and left it in the lock. He turned the knob just enough, then shouldered the shotgun. He aimed low and kicked the door open.

There was nothing there. He went into the living room. The television was on but no one was there—no one and nothing. He saw the opening of the hallway.

"Down the hall, second door on the left," he said to Barrens, who came up beside him.

They went to the hallway, looked down to the other end.

"You stay here," Harker said. "If I miss it, you get it coming out." He turned to Barrens. "You okay?"

"Scared shitless."

"Me, too."

Harker started down the hall, shotgun aimed low. He wished his heart would stop pounding in his ears. He passed a door on the left, then an open bathroom on the right.

He approached the second door on the left wide. It was open and dark inside.

He heard it slurping and sucking in the bedroom.

He leaned forward, peered into the open doorway, and saw it on the bed.

Harker approached the open doorway cautiously, the flashlight held under the barrel of the shotgun. It did not hear him. It kept eating. Standing in the open doorway, he fired.

Its legs shattered on the side nearest Harker, and the spider tumbled off the bed.

Harker rushed forward as he racked the shotgun.

What was left of it was on its back and the legs that remained twitched and pumped.

Harker fired again.

The spider's body broke in half in a splatter of pale goo.

When he heard Barrens come into the room, Harker said, "Turn on the light."

The light came on and Harker squinted a little. The man on the bed had been opened up, like the others. He was naked, somehow making it worse.

The spider lay in pieces on the floor beside the bed.

Harker's cheeks puffed as he let out a big breath.

"You got it?" Barrens said.

"Got it."

"Holy shit," Barrens said as he looked first at the dead man on the bed, then at the spider on the floor. "Where the hell did *that* come from?"

"I'm not sure, but I've got my suspicions."

Another unit pulled up outside, siren wailing.

Harker took the microphone from his shoulder, depressed the button with his thumb, and said, "Two-oh-six at the scene. I got it. It's dead."

"Ten-four, two-oh-six," Shelly said.

Harker leaned against the wall a moment, feeling weak with relief. He went to the next room and knocked on the door. "Sheriff."

"Is it dead?" the woman said on the other side of the door.

"It's dead, ma'am."

The door's lock clicked, then it was pulled open. She stood there in an enormous robe holding a little girl in her arms, a phone in her hand. "Is my husband dead?" she said.

Harker nodded solemnly and said, "I'm afraid so."

"Okay," she said, "I'll need to call my sister and have her come get my little girl." She turned to the girl. "You wanna go over to Aunt Barbara's and play with Celise?"

The little girl, eyes wide and uncertain, nodded as the woman held the phone out before her and punched buttons with her thumb. She put the phone to her ear and turned around, walked back into the room, then turned and came back out, pacing in and out.

"Hi, Barb, it's me," she said. "I'm sorry for calling so late, but something's happened. You need to come over and get Dana... Harvey's dead... I don't know, something, some animal, some ... *thing*, it came in and ... and ..."

She began to sob. She put the girl down and staggered over to the small bed, sat on the edge and cried.

Harker put the mic to his mouth again and said, "Two-oh-six, dispatch, you'd better get an ambulance out here. I've got a woman here who doesn't look so good. And send the coroner, too."

"Ten-four, two-oh-six."

Barrens came out of the bedroom and approached Harker. "What *was* that thing?" he whispered.

"It was just what it looked like—a spider," Harker said.

"But a spider that big?"

"Yeah. A spider that big."

Twenty-Eight

The sister came and took the little girl.

The ambulance came and took Maxine Pruitt.

Other deputies showed up just to look at the spider. They hadn't believed him, of course, not entirely, and they were all anxious to get a look at it themselves.

Harker did not go back in for a while. He'd seen enough of it. Then the coroner had come.

"You're keeping me busy tonight, Tony," the coroner said. Andy Blevins was a man of fifty-five, medium height, whose love of beer was evident in his round belly. "I had to call in some help. There's a rumor going around that you've been chasing a giant spider. Any truth to that?"

"Come here." He led Blevins down the hall and into the room.

"Just like the others," Blevins said, nodding as he looked at the body on the bed.

"Over here," Harker said.

"Holy mother of Christ," Blevins said casually as he looked down at the spider. His reaction was calm, as Harker had expected. Nothing ruffled Andy Blevins. "This come out of BioGenTech?"

"What makes you say that?"

He shrugged. "I've always been suspicious of that place. They seem awfully secretive for a medical research facility. They've got security up the ass. I tried more than once to get a tour of the place. Never got it."

"Well, to tell you the truth, I can't think of any other explanation," Harker said. "There was an explosion there tonight, and then this thing turns up."

Blevins shook his head and the waddle of skin beneath his chin jiggled back and forth. "Makes you wonder what the hell *else* they're doing in there."

"I can guarantee you there's going to be some kind of investigation after this, that's for sure." He looked down at the spider on the floor. Its guts had splattered in all directions. "And I'll tell you something else," he said with a yawn. "I need to get some sleep."

Twenty-Nine

Rodney awoke to another day, and the odd feeling that he'd dreamed it all. He put on a pair of sweatpants and went out to the kitchen, where he smelled breakfast. Mom had made pancakes. He sat down at the table, still sleepy. His dad was already eating.

"I was listening to the radio in the bathroom," Dad said. "There was nothing about a spider."

It hadn't been a dream.

"Maybe they decided not to report it," he said. "I mean, how many people would believe that?"

"If it's a threat," Mom said as she put a plate of pancakes in front of Rodney, "they should let people know."

"Where's Harry?" Rodney said.

"Your little brother was still up watching movies when I woke up," Mom said. "I had to *make* him go to bed. He was so worked up, I thought maybe he'd been loading up on sugar all night."

"No, he was just excited about the spider," Rodney said.

Dad shook his head. "A spider. You know, I went out and looked at the Mustang."

"I'm sorry, Dad," Rodney said, "but there was nothing I could do."

"I'm just glad you and Heidi are all right," Dad said. "I mean, it's amazing it didn't get to you through the roof."

Mom hugged him from behind, bent down, and kissed his cheek. "You should've got us up and told us what was going on."

Rodney spread butter on the top pancake, then poured maple syrup over the stack. "Maybe they killed it," he said. "Maybe that's why it wasn't on the radio."

"Let's hope so," Dad said.

"I'll call the sheriff's office when I'm done here and ask them," Rodney said.

"You're shoveling that in," Mom said. "The sheriff's office isn't going away, it'll be there when you're done. Slow down."

Rodney wanted to know—had they killed it? If so, what had they done with it? Harry was going to want to see it, he was sure.

"I can't wait," he said, standing. He went to the wall phone by the back door. The phonebook was on a small table below the phone, along with a cup full of pens, a pad of Post-its, and a rubber-banded stack of coupons Mom had been saving. He looked up the sheriff's number. It was an old phone, the kind with a long curly cord attaching the receiver to the base. He took the receiver off its hook and punched in the number.

"Sheriff's Department," a woman said.

"Hi, is Sheriff Harker in?" Rodney said.

"Not yet. Can I take a message?"

"This is Rodney Lepke calling. I was wondering ... um, did they kill the spider?"

There was a brief silence over the line. "Who is this, again?"

"Rodney Lepke. I'm one of the teenagers who was down at Lovers' Lookout last night when the spider attacked and, um, killed Tiffany Huff."

"Um, yes, as a matter of fact, the spider was killed last night."

Rodney found it difficult to conceal his excitement. "What have they done with it?"

"Uh, I think you'll have to ask the sheriff himself about that. I'm not sure when I expect him in this morning. Would you like me to have him call you?"

"Yes, please." Rodney gave her his number, hung up the phone, and went back to the table. "They killed it."

"Good," Dad said.

"I can't believe we're talking about … well, a giant spider," Mom said as she sat down at the table with her plate.

Rodney chuckled. "I can't believe I'm talking about it so calmly now. I mean, last night, it almost killed us." He ate for a while, then said, "I'm taking Heidi to the drive-in tonight, if that's okay."

"You need money?" Dad said.

"No, I'm fine."

"Why don't you bring Heidi over for dinner some evening," Mom said.

"Sure, Mom."

"The insurance will cover the damage on the Mustang," Dad said. "I know a guy who'll give me a deal on the roof."

"What are you going to tell the insurance company?" Rodney said. "That the car was attacked by a giant spider?"

Dad smiled. "No. We'll tell them it was vandalism."

"Will they believe it?" Mom said.

"Of course they'll believe it," Dad said. "A lot sooner than they'd believe a story about a giant spider."

Rodney finished his pancakes and poured himself a cup of coffee, then took it to his room. He put it on his nightstand and sat down on the bed, took the phone from the nightstand, and punched in Heidi's number.

"They killed it," he said when she answered.

"How do you know?"

"I called the sheriff's office and asked. They killed it last night. That's all I know right now. Sheriff Harker's supposed to call me back when he gets in."

She released a long sigh of relief. "I didn't get much sleep last night. It's all I could think about—that thing being out there somewhere."

"I know what you mean. I didn't sleep well. We still going to the movie tonight?"

"Yeah."

"Good. What're you doing today?"

"I promised Mom I'd help her do some spring cleaning."

"Sounds like fun."

"Yeah. Lucky me. How about you?"

"I don't know. Harry's still in bed. Mom said he was still up watching movies when she got up this morning."

"Poor kid."

"I guess I'll have to wait till tonight to see you, then."

"Yeah, I'm sorry." She laughed. "You wanted to see me today, too?"

"Whenever possible."

She laughed again. "Maybe I can finish up early with Mom."

"Call me if you do, okay?"

"I will."

Rodney replaced the receiver and yawned. He went into the living room and idly watched *The Jerry Springer Show.*

Thirty

Harker no longer needed the alarm to wake up at six a.m. because he'd been doing it for so long that it happened automatically. But he set the alarm, anyway, just in case. Its irritating buzz sounded a long time that Wednesday morning. He rose up out of his deep sleep slowly, sat on the edge of the bed for a while, and willed himself to wake up. It was going to be a busy day and he'd need all his faculties, but he hadn't slept enough.

An hour later, still feeling weary and heavy after three cups of coffee, he grabbed his keys and wallet and headed outside. He locked the front door on his way out and got into his pickup truck. As he drove away from his house, he turned on the radio. It was already tuned to the news/talk station. They were talking politics—nobody was talking about a giant spider.

That was the first good thing of the day. It meant the story hadn't leaked. Not yet. That gave him a little time to do something—like figure out what to do. He could have someone track down a biology professor from the college in Newbury. It would be easier, though, to get someone from BioGenTech to come over to the station for a look at the spider. He'd spoken to three people from BioGenTech in the early morning hours, before he'd gone to bed. They had not included the CEO, who had been vacationing in Canada. The CEO had been called and Harker had been told he was on his way home.

They were keeping the spider's remains in the garage out back under close guard. No one was allowed in the garage unless personally cleared by Harker.

He parked his truck and went into the station. He stepped into the dispatch room, where there were two on duty—Janice to take the emergency calls, and Angie to take all the others.

"I need a couple things, Angie," he said. "I need to talk to the head of the biology department at the college. Have we heard from the BioGenTech CEO yet? What's his name again?"

"Rexler. No, not yet, but I've been told we will very soon. I'll call the college right now."

He went to his office and checked his messages, each written on a blue slip of paper. Mostly reporters, except for one—Rodney Lepke wanted him to call. The boy deserved to hear the truth. Harker just hoped he and his girlfriend could keep their mouths shut for a while.

Harker made the call and Rodney answered.

"Rodney, it's Sheriff Harker."

"Sheriff! You killed it?"

"Yep. Took it out last night at a house over on Sunset."

"What'd it take?"

"A couple shots from the shotgun. I want to thank you and Harry for your help."

"Harry's gonna want to see it," Rodney said. "Would that be possible?"

"Mmm, I seriously doubt it. And that brings me to this—you need to keep this to yourself for a little while."

"Are you kidding? Who'd believe me?"

"As soon as you hear about it on the news, you can tell anyone you want. But for now, keep it quiet."

Shortly after he ended his conversation with Rodney, Roger Rexler called.

"I was told you wanted to talk to me," Rexler said. "About the fire, I imagine."

"It is, but it's not something I can discuss with you over the phone. Would you mind coming over here to the station as soon as possible?"

"I already talked to the deputies," Rexler said. "I told them everything I could, and we're—"

"This is something different. It's very urgent, Mr. Rexler. If you'd prefer, I could send someone to bring you here in a cruiser."

Rexler was at the station twenty minutes later.

He was in his early fifties, fit, medium height, with shivering black hair and a pair of wire-framed glasses. He was dressed casually—a pricey yellow cashmere sweater pulled over a green shirt, black pants, black loafers. He looked ready to hit the links.

"This has not been a good day, Sheriff," Rexler said as he took a seat in front of Harker's desk. "I've had to call the families of those killed in the explosion and fire. To extend my condolences."

"Oh, yes, I'm sure that was difficult for you."

"It wasn't easy. And someone from the parent company is flying in this afternoon. I have my work cut out for me. How is the investigation coming?"

"I talked to the arson investigator earlier, but he had nothing conclusive for me yet. Except that the explosion was apparently centered in a basement lab."

Rexler nodded. "Yes, that's been the result of BioGenTech's investigation, as well."

"What goes on in the basement labs, Mr. Rexler?" Harker asked.

"Well ... I couldn't tell you right off the top of my head. Research programs evolve, they move around the facility."

"I see."

"Is that what you wanted to tell me?"

"No, Mr. Rexler, I want to show you something." Harker stood and walked around his desk. "Come with me out to the garage in back. We found something that I think might have come from that basement lab."

"Oh, really? What's that?"

"I'd rather show it to you."

He led Rexler out the back door and across the parking lot. All four garage doors were closed. Harker opened the door, stepped back, let Rexler go in first. He pulled the door shut, stepped ahead of Rexler, and led him out to the open concrete floor and the thing spread out over it. He watched Rexler's face closely.

When he realized what he was looking at, he immediately stopped walking and took one step back, eyes wide.

They had put the spider back together on the garage floor as if it were a jigsaw puzzle. It lay flat on its belly. It smelled like a compost pile, and the smell was getting worse as the day warmed.

"What the hell is this?" Rexler said as a sickened frown lined his brow.

"It's a sun spider, Mr. Rexler. Ever heard of it? Nasty spider."

"What *is* this?" He turned to Harker and shook his head. "I don't understand, Sheriff Harker."

"They don't usually get this big."

"Why are you showing me this?"

"Because it showed up shortly after the explosion in the basement lab of BioGenTech, Mr. Rexler."

Rexler's frown disappeared and his face smoothed out. He looked at Harker that way for several long seconds. "Is this a joke, Sheriff?"

"No, it's not."

"Are you trying to say this … this creature came from BioGenTech?"

"I am."

"Do you have some kind of *proof*?"

"I don't. Not yet. But I want you to know that I know."

"Are you charging me with something, Sheriff?"

"Not right now. But think about it, Mr. Rexler. On the one hand, we've got a big explosion at a place called BioGenTech, a so-called medical research facility that has more security than a military installation, and on the other hand, I've suddenly got a giant spider killing people right and left. A *giant spider*—something that does not exist in nature, not without the help of, say, scientists playing around with genes and test tubes. The connection *does* offer itself up, don't you think?"

"If this is all you have to say to me, I think I'll be going now." Rexler turned and headed back the way he'd come. He said over his shoulder, "If you have anything more to say, you can say it to our attorneys."

"Thanks for coming out," Harker said with a smile.

Two hours later, Harker had Professor Enid Hayward in the garage. She was a stout woman in her late forties with ash-colored hair, her purse slung over her shoulder. She gawked at the spider for a while, arms spread just a little at her sides.

"This is … this is just …" She shook her head slowly as she stared down at it. Then she turned to Harker and said, "This is a sun spider."

"Yes, it is."

"This is … incredible. It's incredible, Sheriff."

"I thought you might think so."

Professor Hayward walked slowly around the spider's remains, occasionally remarking, "My god," or, "Unbelievable." Finally she turned to Harker again and said, "Where did it come from?"

"Well, that's why I tracked you down today, Professor," Harker said. "I was hoping *you* might have some idea where a thing like this would come from?"

She laughed as she turned to the spider again. "Are you serious, Sheriff?" She looked at it for a while, slowly shaking her head. "This is … so far removed … from anything I've ever … have you notified the authorities?"

"Which authorities would that be?"

"I don't know. The Department of Fish and Game?"

"How about the Orkin Man?" Harker grinned. "Tell me, professor, is this something that ever happens in nature? Something very small becoming … quite big?"

"In nature?" She laughed again. "Not unless I missed some very interesting lectures in college. Nothing like this has ever been recorded, that's for sure." She walked around to the spider's hairy face and crouched down for a better look. "This is fantastic," she whispered.

"Could it possibly be the result of, say, some kind of genetic testing or experimentation?"

"These days, I suppose that's not impossible," she said. She lifted her eyes to him. "Have you talked to anybody over at BioGenTech about this?"

"I'm ahead of you there. I just wanted to make absolutely certain that this sort of thing didn't normally happen." Harker walked over to her and looked down at the spider's face. The four fangs curved out of the bristly face.

Professor Hayward touched one of the top fangs and moved it aside. It made a moist sound.

Harker thought of the fang Rodney had given him. "You know, I have one of those in my desk draw—"

It hit him with such force, he took a step backward.

Harker did not know how he had missed it for so long. He'd looked at the dead spider a dozen times or more, looked right at it, and it hadn't hit him, he hadn't made the connection.

This spider had all four fangs, none were missing. There was still another spider out there.

"Tell me something, professor," Harker said, working to keep his voice level. "If a sun spider were to lose one of its fangs, would a new fang grow back?"

"No, it wouldn't."

Harker took a deep breath and let it out slowly.

Professor Hayward stood and said, "Could I get a few pictures of this? I have a camera in my car and I'd like to—"

"Uh, well, now might not be a good time."

She sniffed and said, "It's starting to smell. You won't have it for long."

"I'm afraid we're going to have to go, Professor," Harker said. He went to her side and tugged her elbow. "Come with me, let's go."

She went along with him.

"Do me a favor, Professor," Harker said as they left the garage. "Go home and stay inside. Do you understand?"

She stopped walking and turned to him. "Are you saying this isn't the only one?"

"I'm saying you should go home and stay inside, that's all." He escorted her back into the building and to the front counter. "Thank you so much for coming, Professor," he said as she left. He turned around and hurried into the dispatch room.

He had to let his deputies know.

Thirty-One

Alberta McCormack, Allie to everyone she knew, stood in her kitchen and watched her husband Sidney pulling weeds in his garden out front. He'd turned half the front yard into a vegetable garden. He planted every spring, then nursed the plants along. The vegetables they got from the garden tasted far better than anything from the store, and they saved money.

She made sandwiches at the kitchen counter while music played on the radio on top of the refrigerator. She and Sid were both in their mid-seventies, but they still listened to rock and roll, and usually kept their FM radios tuned to a classic rock station. She hummed along with "White Rabbit" by Jefferson Airplane.

They had been had met at a commune a thousand years ago, back when they were middle-aged hippies, he a certified public accountant, she a grammar schoolteacher, both escaping their lives in a world of beads and sex and acid and protests. A lot of the young hippies hadn't known what to make of them at first because they didn't trust anyone over thirty, and Allie and Sid were *in* their thirties. But they'd gotten through all that eventually, and when they came out the other side, they ended up cutting their hair, bathing, going back to work, getting married, and having kids. They bought a house in Ridgeton in which they'd lived for almost thirty years. She'd stayed home to raise the kids. Sid had been made a senior partner at the accounting firm where he'd worked for twelve years. Allie had gone back to work for a while, once the kids were old enough. But it just wasn't the same anymore. She had come to enjoy her life as a housewife and found it very fulfilling, more so than teaching.

Their kids, both boys, Robert and Scott, had grown up and moved out, and were married with children of their own. Allie thought herself lucky to have them living nearby. But once they were gone, the house in Ridgeton seemed much too big for just Allie and Sid. They'd stayed there until Sid retired, then bought a deluxe double-wide mobile home and moved into Pineway Mobile Home Estates in Hope Valley, where they'd been ever since. It was a seniors-only development and often seemed half-filled with grandchildren using the pool and running all over the place. She especially enjoyed the summer months when grandchildren visited more frequently, and the narrow little streets that wound through Pineway Mobile Home Estates were filled with their laughter.

Sid always looked so content when he worked in his garden. There were two windows side by side above the kitchen sink and counter, and Allie occasionally looked out the one in front of her as she spread low-fat mayonnaise on slices of seven-grain bread, then French's mustard, and topped that with butter lettuce—iceberg irritated Sid's diverticulosis.

Sid liked the Deli-Fresh sliced oven-roasted turkey on his sandwiches, while Allie preferred the honey-roasted ham. She made one sandwich of each. She sliced up a tomato—store-bought, unfortunately—and put a slice on each sandwich, added a slice of Tillamook cheddar, and placed a slice of bread on top of each. She put the sandwiches on paper plates and cut them both in half. She watched as Sid walked out of sight and around the mobile home, headed for the patio outside their back door.

Danny and Maris Zimmer's little dog Pepe was yipping his head off out in the front yard. It was bad enough to hear Pepe's yipping in the night from a few homes away, but Sid got irate when the tiny dog came down and stood staring at him with those big, bulgy eyes, seeming to yip at him and no one else. It was a Chihuahua, but it was small even for that breed. It looked like a *toy* Chihuahua, if such a breed existed. Pepe would make his way to the back yard, where he would stare and yip at Sid.

Sid insisted it was not really a dog, but that the Zimmers had shaved their hamster, which was now rabid.

Allie hoped she could get out there in time to chase Pepe off before he soured Sid's mood. He'd seemed rather buoyant at breakfast that morning, and he'd kissed her three times. In recent weeks, he'd made some remarks about writing a book, a novel about their time in the commune.

"Oh, you wouldn't," she'd said.

"Why not?"

"You wouldn't use my real *name,* or anything, would you?"

He'd laughed. "Of course not. It's a novel, I'm just drawing on my past experience to tell a fictional story."

"What an embarrassing experience."

"Why are you embarrassed by it? We were young and idealistic."

"Sid, we were drunk and stoned and we had sex a lot, with a *lot* of different people."

"So, we got laid a lot, we were still idealistic. I want to get that across in the book."

He'd mentioned it a few other times, too. She wondered if he'd decided to go ahead and write it. It would be very cool if he ended up sitting on a bestseller. It was a nice fantasy, anyway. He'd never written fiction before, but he was an elegant, well-spoken man, and she had no doubt that Sid had it in him to write a book.

Pepe yipped from the side of the house. He was slowly making his way to the back.

She ripped open a bag of Lays potato chips and put a handful on each paper plate. She put the plates on a round tray of brown plastic, along with a cold can of Diet Shasta grape soda for Sid, and a can of Diet Dr Pepper for her, and a paper towel for each of them.

Holding the tray with both hands, Allie went down the short hall through the laundry room, where a small washer and dryer hunkered side by side, to the back door. She balanced the tray as she reached out and opened the door. It swung out as she stepped onto the small wooden landing atop four wooden steps that led down to the concrete.

Somehow she managed to hang on to the tray without spilling anything in spite of what she saw when she stepped out the door. Later, she would wonder how she'd done that.

Sid was stretched out on his back on the concrete. The thing that straddled him with its many legs had its face buried in Sid's abdomen. It made wet bubbling sounds as it slurped and sucked.

The panic that rose into her constricted throat filled her lungs, but she did not scream. Instead, she took a step backward into the open door.

Pepe appeared at the corner of the house, yipping his head off. The tiny dog saw the spider and immediately attacked. He ran to the spider and bit one of its front legs, then backed up and yip-yip-yipped.

The spider was on Pepe before the dog had time to cry out.

As it gobbled up the Chihuahua with its three huge black fangs, Allie backed into the trailer and closed the door. Her knees wobbled beneath her as she went back into the kitchen and put the tray on the counter. She hurried into the living room and grabbed the phone on the end table beside Sid's recliner. She dropped it, picked it up, and clutched it tightly in her hand.

Her heart raced as she turned on the phone and punched in nine-one-one.

"Nine-one-one, what is your emergency?" a woman said.

Allie did not hesitate for a moment, did not care how it sounded. "There's a giant spider in my back yard, and it's eating my husband."

"Where are you located?" the woman said.

"Two-twelve Pineway Mobile Home Estates."

"Where is the spider now?"

Allie hurried back to the laundry room and looked out the small window beside the door.

Sid lay on the patio, opened up and partially eaten, like a piece of roadkill. She could not see the spider.

"I don't see it anymore," Allie said as she cried, as tears rolled down her cheeks. "It's moved."

She went to the living room and knelt on the couch to look out the window behind it.

"There it is!" she said. "Oh, my God, it's going over to Doretta Claub's house."

"Okay, listen, ma'am, we're sending units over there now, but you need to stay inside, all right? Do *not* go outside. Call your neighbors and tell *them* not to go outside. Do you understand?"

"Yes, yes, I'll call Doretta right now."

Thirty-Two

The spider made its way across Spruce Street, but when it reached Doretta Claub's trailer, it veered right and kept going down the street.

It crawled over the two pink flamingos in Stan and Bonita Lodge's yard and knocked the colorful pinwheels out of the large redwood plant box at the end of Herman Shore's trailer.

It turned left and went down Sycamore Street, where it followed the road for a while before cutting off to the right and going through Paul and Justine Marx's front yard. A dog inside the Marxes' trailer barked furiously as the spider went by.

It collapsed a small picket fence that ran along the back of the yard, then went into Tom and Regina Racine's front yard and on to Peach Tree Street. On the other side of Peach Tree stood the tan cinderblock wall that went all around the development.

The spider climbed the wall with no effort and left the park.

Thirty-Three

When Harker arrived at the McCormacks' trailer, the ambulance was there, and a deputy had already gone inside. He got out of his cruiser, shotgun in hand, and approached the two EMTs who stood talking at the rear of the ambulance.

"They don't need us," one said. "They need the coroner." Harker knew his name was Steve, but he didn't know his last name. Harker didn't know the other guy.

He saw a body lying on a concrete patio in the trailer's back yard. The man's clothes were torn up … and so was the man.

"What's up?" Harker said.

"You need to see this," Steve said. "He was dead before we got here. We knew better than to touch a thing."

"I appreciate that, guys," Harker said. "You see or hear anything?"

They shook their heads and the one Harker didn't know said, "Just the old lady talking about a giant spider." He chuckled nervously.

"Is that right?" Harker said, giving away nothing with his poker face.

The guy nodded and said, "Yeah. A giant spider. You believe that?"

"Well, you guys can go, I guess," Harker said. "We'll get the coroner down here."

"Okay, Sheriff," Steve said as he headed for the driver's door.

Harker turned and started toward the body when the guy he didn't know spoke.

"Wait, Sheriff," he said. "What is it? What *did* that?" He was trying to smile, but his fear showed in it, and for a moment, he looked as if he were pulling back the corners of his mouth in a grimace.

"We're not sure yet," Harker said. "But stay inside unless absolutely necessary." Then he went over to the body.

The guy got in the ambulance, and Steve drove away.

Harker looked down at the body, but only for a moment. He walked around to the front of the trailer. The door was open and he heard sobbing. He went up the front steps and stood in the doorway. Deputy Cheryl Hainey sat beside an old woman on the couch. The old woman sobbed into the palm of her hand.

"Have you called anyone?" Hainey said. "A relative, maybe? Someone who can come over and be with you?"

The old woman shook her head.

"Would you like me to call someone? Do you have any children in the area?"

She nodded. "Cuh-could you … call my son?" she said.

"Sure, sure," Hainey said.

"Ma'am, I'm Sheriff Harker. Would you mind if I come in and ask you a few questions?"

She nodded and tried to collect herself. As Harker came inside, she said, "It was a spider, Sheriff. I know how it sounds, I know it sounds crazy, but it was a giant spider, it was—"

"Calm down, Ma'am. I believe you. Did you get a good look at it?"

She nodded again.

"Did you happen to notice if it was missing a fang?"

"I-I saw fangs, but ..." She shook her head. "No, I'm sorry, I didn't notice how many it had."

"Did you see which way it went?"

"It went that way," she said pointing to her left. She took a tissue from a box in her lap, dabbed her eyes and cheeks with it.

"What's in that direction in the park?" Harker said.

"Well, you go far enough and you hit the wall."

"The wall," Harker said, mostly to himself. Providing it had kept going in that direction, it might have gone over the wall and left the park already. He hadn't seen it on the way in, or he would've stopped. He needed deputies to check out the park. There was a chance it could still be somewhere within its walls. He took the microphone clipped to the shoulder of his shirt and pressed down the button with his thumb. "Two-oh-six, I need backup at Pineway Mobile Home Estates, space two-twelve, that's space two-twelve at Pineway Mobile Home Estates. And send the coroner over here, too."

Deputy Hainey said, "I didn't see it, Sheriff. I've been watching for it, like you said, but I didn't see it. She did, though," she said, nodding at the old woman.

"Take her statement after you've called her son," Harker said. He turned to the old woman. "I'm sorry for your loss, ma'am." He turned and left the trailer.

Backup arrived—three units. Harker sent them through the park and told them to have their shotguns ready.

The coroner arrived a few minutes later.

"Tony, this looks very familiar," Blevins said as he approached Harker. "This is what happened to the people from last night. Exactly, in fact." He stood over the body and nodded as he looked down at it. "Exactly."

Harker told him there was another spider running loose.

Blevin's bushy white eyebrows went up and he said, "You shitting me?"

"I shit you not. The remaining spider has only three fangs. It lost one when it bit a seventy-two Mustang in the trunk."

Blevins went to the back of the hearse, where his young male assistant had pulled out the unpadded metal gurney. He returned with a body bag and opened it beside the body on the ground. He rolled the body into the bag, drew it together, and zipped it up.

They put the old man on the gurney and the assistant wheeled the bagged corpse back to the hearse and shoved it inside.

"To be honest, Tony," Blevins said, "I'm having a little trouble getting my mind around this, you know what I'm saying? I mean ... a giant spider."

"I know exactly what you're saying. We're all having that problem. Wait till you *see* it. Your mind has to get around it pretty damned quick when you *see* it."

Blevins laughed a low, humorless chuckle. "You sure there's only one more?"

Harker sighed as a sickening feeling moved through his stomach. "I *hope* there's only one more." He patted the coroner on the shoulder. "Stay inside, Andy. And keep all of this to yourself for now. I don't want it to get out any sooner than necessary, because as soon as it does, this all turns into a circus."

"I understand."

The deputies returned from their patrol of the park. None of them had seen the spider.

"It moves very fast," Harker said, frustration in his voice. "It could cover a whole lot of ground in no time. We can't even *guess* where it is." He got in his car and got on the radio. "All units, cover the town. It's the only thing we can do right now."

Dispatch said, "I got the press here asking about giant spiders, and I'm getting lots of sightings."

"Where's the last one?" Harker said.

"Thirty-nine West Pearl Street. The call just came in. A Mr. Mike O'Ryan."

Harker looked up at the deputies gathered at his open door. "Let's hit it, that's just up the road."

They got in their cars and left the park, going over the twenty-five-miles-per-hour speed limit.

Thirty-Four

Sandy Chatsworth was home from work with a bad cold. She worked at the Wells Fargo Bank on Center Street in Hope Valley. Her son Zack was outside playing in the front yard, her husband Leo down at the office selling insurance. Sandy lay on the couch with a blanket over her and her favorite pillow under her head, watching a cooking show.

The front door opened and Zack came inside. He was seven years old and beautiful, with his father's blond hair and strong features. It never ceased to amaze Sandy that she felt an almost crippling surge of love every time she looked at him.

"Mom, can I go 'cross the street to the park and play on the swings?" he said, standing before the couch, between Sandy and the television.

Her sinuses were congested, and when she spoke, her voice was scratchy. "No, honey, you know you can't go over there unless Daddy or I go with you, and I'm just too sick to go today. I'm sorry, honey."

"S'okay," he said. He joined his hands in front of him and said, "Can I get you something?"

There was that surge of love again. It filled Sandy's chest to bursting—there was actually a moment when she felt as if the T-shirt she wore were too tight. She held out her arms and said,

"C'mere." She held him to her and squeezed. "I hope you don't get my cold."

"If I got your cold," Zack said, "could I stay home when school starts again next week?"

"If you get my cold, you'll have to, silly."

He stepped back, threw up his arms, and jumped as he said, "Yippee! No school! I hope I get your cold."

Zack turned and ran back to the front door, pulling it closed as he went outside.

Sandy sat up on the couch and looked out the plate-glass window behind it to the front yard. Zack wheeled his pedal-car around on the front lawn, and a huge golden spider appeared and pounced on the boy.

"Zack!" Sandy screamed.

She shot from the sofa, ran to the front door, and opened it. She kicked the screen door open and threw herself outside.

The spider's back was to Sandy as it went to work on Zack. She ran screaming toward the spider and, just as it started to turn around, jumped on its back. She pounded it with her fists, clawed at it with her fingernails.

The spider backed up, turned left, then right, trying to dislodge her, but she held tightly onto the thick hairs that grew on its back. She gouged its closest eye with all four fingers, and her hand punched through the bubble-like surface and sank into white mush. It reared up and Sandy tried to hold on, but her grip slipped away and she slid off the spider's back.

She hit the ground with a grunt, opened her eyes, and saw that she lay just a few feet from Zack. She crawled on hands and knees to his side. He did not move, just stared up at the sky with foggy eyes. His clothes were torn. Blood was smeared all over him and she realized his right arm lay next to him, unattached, severed at the elbow.

"My baby!" she cried. "My baby! My baby!"

The spider's front legs pressed in on her from both sides. The sharp hooks in the legs dug into the flesh of her upper arms. She felt its fangs sink into her back. Sandy was spared excruciating pain by a quick death.

Thirty-Five

Blind in one eye, the spider zigged and zagged out of the Chatworths' front lawn and crossed the street.

A man stepped out onto his front porch with a rifle. He fired at the spider and hit a leg on its blind side. The spider became a blur as it left the neighborhood, following West Pearl Street. It swerved onto the shoulder and sped along the ditch to avoid oncoming cars.

Other drivers knew something had passed them, but it was moving so fast, they couldn't tell what it was.

The spider veered further away from the road and disappeared into the woods.

Thirty-Six

When Harker got out of his car, Mike O'Ryan of 39 West Pearl Street was standing on his front porch, rifle in hand.

"I took a shot at it," O'Ryan said as Harker approached. "I think I hit it, too. It ran off."

"Which way did it go?" Harker said.

"West on Pearl," O'Ryan said, pointing. "It got the lady across the street," he said, pointing again, "and her little boy."

Harker followed O'Ryan's pointing finger with his eyes and saw the bodies lying on the front lawn across the street. He saw a lot of blood and didn't want to go over there.

Harker turned to the approaching deputies and said, "Deputy Whitman, take Mr. O'Ryan's statement and call the coroner for the people across the street. The rest of you, we're going after it. West on Pearl. Keep those shotguns ready."

He got back into his car and headed south. He flipped on his siren and lights and sped down the road, eyes moving back and forth, looking for some sign of the spider, or better, the spider itself.

He led the other deputies past a large stretch of woods on the right, then on into town.

Harker saw nothing.

Once in town, he turned onto Center Street, then got on the radio. "Looks like we lost it. Just keep covering the town, even if we have to drive around all day and night. It was heading this way. Any recent sightings?"

"Pearl Street was the last one," Dispatch said.

"Okay. We just keep looking."

They watchfully drove the streets of downtown Hope Valley. There were no more calls about the spider.

The afternoon's shadows grew long, but the spider did not show itself.

PART THREE

Creature Feature

Thirty-Seven

After dressing for his date with Heidi, Rodney left his room to find Mom setting the table for dinner in the dining room.

"You don't mind if I take the Toyota, Mom?" he said.

"No, of course not," she said. "It's still too cold at night for you to be driving around with a big hole in your roof. Let me get the key for you." She went to her purse, which was always on the small table beside the front door, took out her keys, slid the key off the ring, gave it to him, and kissed his cheek. "Have fun and be careful."

He went out to the garage. He'd moved the Mustang to the curb so he could get out, then got into Mom's Camry and backed out of the garage.

Harry had been upset with Rodney for giving the sheriff the sun spider's fang. He wanted to keep it. Rodney had promised him he would go to the sheriff's office tomorrow and ask for the fang back. Harry was a pessimist and doubted he would never see it again.

"What would the sheriff want with a spider fang?" Rodney had said to Harry that afternoon.

"He probably wants it as a souvenir, like me."

"Yeah, but I didn't *tell* him I was giving it to him."

"That probably doesn't matter. He probably thinks you gave it to him."

Rodney shook his head and rolled his eyes. "Why do you *always* see the dark side of everything?"

"Because that's usually the side that wins," Harry said. "I'm a realist."

"You're eleven years old, you shouldn't even *know* the word 'realist.'"

He'd finally gotten Harry to agree that he would not give up hope until tomorrow, after Rodney'd had a chance to ask for the fang back.

Rodney drove across town to Cutter Way, and on to Wooded Acres.

Heidi's house reminded Rodney of a ski lodge—it even had an A-frame roof. He rang the bell and she opened the door a few seconds later. She put her purse strap up over her shoulder, then leaned forward and gave him a quick kiss. Then she stepped out of the doorway and pulled the door closed.

In the car, he said, "You didn't want me to meet your parents?"

She laughed. "Nah, I figured you could do without the stress. You can meet them later, preferably when we're not on a date. That just adds tension to the date, don't you think?"

"Flattery will get you everywhere."

"Really?"

"Oh, yeah."

"Then … you're very smart … and very funny … and very well-dressed."

They laughed as he pulled her close and kissed her. The kiss became intense and their embrace tightened. Finally, Heidi laughed and pulled away gently.

"It's not good to make out on an empty stomach," she said. "C'mon, let's get some pizza."

"But if we eat, then we'll have to wait an hour before we can start making out again."

"That's *swimming*."

"Oh. Okay."

Dube's Deli had the best pizza in Hope Valley. It was a take-and-bake, but they also offered the option of having it cooked there. They went into the deli and discussed toppings.

"I love everything but bell peppers," Heidi said.

"Me, too," Rodney said. "I like ..." He stopped, sighed, then rolled his eyes and steeled himself to the inevitable response. "I like anchovies."

"Me, *too*!" she said, eyes widening.

"No shit?"

"No shit!"

"A woman who likes anchovies?" he said. "Will you marry me?"

She laughed and slipped her arm around his waist, her fingers into his back pocket.

They ordered a combination pizza *with* anchovies, then took it with them to the NightLight Drive-in Theater. Rodney paid admission at the gate, then drove onto the hilly lot. They went up and down the broad humps for a while until he picked a spot and parked.

The sky was a bleeding wound along the tops of the mountains in the west. Shadows had lengthened, bled together into one and now blanketed everything.

"I can't believe I agreed to come see a scary movie," Heidi said.

"You don't like them?"

"I hate them. They give me nightmares. Bad ones. I'm serious."

"I believe you."

"Don't they bother you?"

He shrugged. "Yeah, they scare me sometimes. But that's why I like them. I can get scared and not be in any danger. I'm lazy, I guess."

She laughed.

Rodney turned on the radio and tuned to 1140 AM. An old Buddy Holly song was playing. It was broadcast from the movie theater, and all they ever played before the movie started were oldies from the 1950s.

Heidi held the pizza and a stack of napkins on her lap. She removed the napkins from the top of the box and opened it. Dube's provided paper plates if you asked, and she'd gotten two. They were on the seat between her and Rodney.

"Okay, hand me your plate," she said. She put two slices of pizza on his plate and handed it back with a clump of napkins.

"Smell them anchovies," Rodney said before biting into a piece.

"It's been a long time since I've had anchovies," Heidi said.

"Me, too! Nobody else ever wants them, so I never get them. I mean, I never just buy a pizza for myself."

"Maybe you should," she said. "Every once in a while, I get one of those little personal pizzas from Round Table, up the street from my house. Just to be able to have anchovies."

"We're a sad and put-upon minority, we anchovy lovers," Rodney said. He chewed for a while, then said, "This is delicious."

A Bugs Bunny cartoon came on the big screen. Rodney and Heidi laughed at the rabbit's antics as they ate. After that, an advertisement for the snack bar came on, with dancing drinks and singing buckets of popcorn frolicking across the screen.

"I'm full," Rodney said.

"Me, too," Heidi said.

"You only had one piece."

"It doesn't take much to satisfy me. How many did you have?"

"Four."

"I guess it takes more to satisfy you. I'll have to keep that in mind." She bobbed one eyebrow suggestively, then laughed. She closed the lid on the pizza box and put it on the floorboard.

Rodney reached into the back seat and grabbed the pillow there, held it up between them, and said, "I brought our pillow along." He placed it between the seat backs. "Unless you'd rather get in the back seat."

"No, the back seat's got that big hump in the middle," she said. "This is fine."

They moved both their seats all the way back, then reclined in them. They kissed for a while, then looked up when the movie started.

"We don't have to watch if you don't want," Rodney said.

"No, I don't mind," she said. "*You* wanna see this movie, right?"

"Hey, if I have to choose between you and a movie, the movie loses. Every time." They kissed again, moving their hands over each other's body.

A few minutes later, she gently pulled away and took a deep breath. "Oh, look," she said, pointing at the screen. "Bare titties."

Rodney lifted his head.

A woman wearing only panties ran through an old, creepy hotel. She ducked into a room, closed the door, and locked it.

Rodney had read about the movie in *Fangoria* magazine and knew the basic plot. Of course, when it came to plot, one slasher movie kind of blurred into all the others. There was little chance of being surprised. Rodney didn't expect it to be any good—very few body-count films were. But then, he didn't plan on watching it.

"The killer's somewhere in the room with her," Heidi whispered. "I can tell by the creepy music."

The girl turned and the music came up as a black-gloved hand plunged a knife deep into her left eye in close-up.

Heidi screamed and buried her face in Rodney's shoulder. "Oh, it's *gory,* too. I *hate* gory movies."

"What'd you expect from something called *Thrill Killer*?" Rodney said with a smile. He turned her face up and kissed her again. "By the way, the only bare titties I'm interested in are yours."

"You're a boob man, huh?"

"Yep." He lifted her sweater, put his face between her braless breasts, and squeezed them together. Heidi laughed as he locked his lips over her sternum and blew air noisily.

Rodney lost track of time as they lay there holding each other and kissing. The movie's soundtrack played on the radio but was nothing more than white noise to him. He slipped his hand beneath her sweater, exhilarated by the feel of her skin, so warm and smooth and pleasing to the touch.

A horn honked near the front of the theater lot.

Heidi lifted her arms and took the sweater off over her head. Rodney put his mouth on her right breast, sucked on her nipple, ran his tongue over it.

Another horn honked in a different part of the lot. Then another. And another.

Rodney lifted his head and looked to the front of the lot. He saw nothing out of the ordinary and started to turn back to Heidi, but he did a double take.

"Oh, my god," he said as he stared at the screen. He sat up and hit the lever to bring the seat upright again.

Heidi did the same. "What?" she said.

"Look at the screen," he said. "It's on the screen. I thought it was supposed to be *dead*."

The spider crawled across the screen in a zigzag pattern. The movie was projected onto the spider's back as it scurried over the screen, casting a dark shadow just beneath it.

"Oh, my god," Rodney said. "There's more than one."

Thirty-Eight

The spider crawled over the face of the onscreen actress, turned around and crawled back a bit. Then it turned around again, went to the end of the screen and crawled around to the back, where it disappeared from sight.

Rodney felt a growing sense of panic. He looked around the lot a moment until his gaze fell on the small cinderblock building in the center—the snack bar. He needed a phone. He started the car, pulled out of the slot, and turned right. He drove between two long humps of pavement and went to the snack bar. He pulled up directly in front of its door.

"You stay here," Rodney said. "I'm going in there to call the sheriff."

He got out of the car and went into the snack bar.

It was a dreary place. One of the fluorescent bars of light overhead flickered annoyingly. The tile floor was filthy. The counter and candy display case were painted a bright, festive orange, but the walls were a dull and faded yellow.

Rodney went to the counter. There was no one on the other side. Behind the counter was an open door. He waited.

A skinny young man in his early twenties came out of the open doorway. He was pale with shaggy black hair and a little tuft of whiskers between his lower lip and chin.

"What can I get for you?" he said.

"I need to use your phone," Rodney said. He saw the phone beside the cash register.

"What's this for?" the guy said.

"It's an emergency, can I use it?"

"There's a payphone out by the—"

"I don't have any change!" Rodney said with urgency. "I have to make a call *right now*."

"Is it local?"

"*Yes*, it's local."

The guy nodded toward the phone. "Okay, go ahead, but make it quick. What's the emergency?"

"A giant spider." Rodney picked up the phone and punched in nine-one-one.

The guy on the other side of the counter nodded without expression. "Came out of a flying saucer, I suppose?"

Rodney ignored him.

"Nine-one-one, what's your emergency?" the female voice said on the line.

"Listen, I'm at the NightLight Drive-in, and there's a spider here. I just saw it crawl across the screen. This is Rodney Lepke—tell Sheriff Harker who I am. And get somebody over here right away. I'm at the snack bar now, but I don't think I'm going to stick around."

Rodney hung up the phone and turned to the shaggy guy who stood staring at Rodney agape on the other side of the counter.

"Are you serious?" the guy said.

"Yes. I'm getting the hell out of here." Rodney turned and went back to his car.

Thirty-Nine

"Two-oh-six, two-oh-six, I received a call from a Rodney Lepke. He says it's at the NightLight Drive-in Theater. It crawled across the screen. Lepke says he's at the snack bar."

Harker grabbed the radio's microphone as he drove along Magnolia Street, watchful and slow. "I'm on my way," he said. "All units, meet me at the NightLight Drive-in Theater, *all* units."

He flipped on the siren and lights and pressed his foot down on the accelerator.

Forty

The spider crawled across the back of the movie screen, then dropped to the ground again. It scurried along the western fence, a tall, brown, wooden fence that stood about eight feet tall. It would have been no problem to go over the fence, but the spider chose to skitter alongside it instead.

The ends of its legs thumped the ground firmly with every step.

It moved away from the fence and crawled over a car. Someone inside screamed as the spider went off the rear of the car, and then crawled onto the hood of the next car in the row, a Ford Taurus.

The driver's-side door opened and a young man got out, saying, "What the fuck?"

By the time the young man looked to see who or what was on the roof of the car, the spider had gotten off the car in back. It came around the corner of the car and reared up at him. Only in those last seconds did the man cry out. The cry was cut short when the creature sank its top fang into his chest, shattering through his ribs, and its bottom fangs into his lower abdomen.

It ate for a little while, loudly and wetly, ignoring the screams that rose around it. It left its food behind half-eaten and went along the wall again toward the gate. It stopped at the gate and turned to a Toyota Camry on its way out.

Forty-One

"Oh, shit!" Rodney shouted as Heidi screamed.

The spider started to climb up onto the hood of the car.

Rodney put the car in reverse and hit the gas. As he backed up, the spider slid off the hood and onto the ground.

"Son of a *bitch,*" Rodney said as he backed up further, then stopped. He turned right and headed back to the snack bar. He kept looking in his rearview mirror, but the spider did not follow.

He heard the sirens in the distance, rapidly getting closer.

"What're we gonna do?" Heidi said.

Rodney reached over and took her hand. "Don't worry, we'll be fine. We won't get out of the car." As he parked in front of the snack bar again, he wished he had a gun, or even a club, *something*.

Blue and red lights pulsed in his rearview mirror, and he saw a patrol car heading toward him. It pulled up beside him and Rodney and Sheriff Harker rolled down their windows.

"When did you see it last?" Harker said.

"Just a minute ago at the gate," Rodney said. "It jumped on the car, but I shook it off."

"Did you see it leave the lot?"

"I don't know if it left or not."

"Damn," Harker muttered. He put his radio mic to his mouth and said, "All units, set up a perimeter around the drive-in theater, and watch out for it. It's still here somewhere. Inside or outside, I'm not sure. But I want a perimeter around the theater, and if you see it, kill it." He put the microphone back on its rack. "You going to stick around, Rodney?"

"I'm afraid to move," Rodney said, and he meant it. He was afraid to stay because of the spider, and he was afraid to try to leave, again because of the spider.

"You might want to go into the snack bar and close the door until I tell you it's safe," Harker said.

Rodney nodded. "We'll think about it."

Harker killed the engine, took the shotgun from between the seats, and got out of his cruiser. He went into the snack bar.

Rodney turned to Heidi and said, "You wanna go into the snack bar and wait for them to kill it?" He jerked his head back toward the gate and said, "Or would you rather try to make a run for it?"

"I don't know," she said. "What do you think?"

"Well ..." He thought about it a moment. "There's liable to be shooting out here. And I'd rather not try to drive out of here and run into that thing again."

"I agree," she said. "Let's go inside."

Rodney opened the door and got out, went around the front of the car, and joined Heidi at the open doorway to the snack bar. He nodded for her to go in first, then followed.

Harker turned to them when they entered. The door opened inward and was propped against the wall inside with a rock the size of a football. Harker kicked the rock aside and closed the old wooden door. Posters for smoothies, curly-fries, and Coca-Cola decorated the walls on both sides.

"Hey, what're you doing?" the guy behind the counter said.

"I'm closing the door." He turned to the thin, pale guy by the register. "There's a spider out there the size of a Hyundai, and believe me, you do *not* want it to come in here. If it does, you're dead. I don't suppose you've got a gun in here, do you?"

The guy shook his head. "All I got is this," he said as he produced an aluminum baseball bat from behind the counter.

Rodney turned to Heidi and she stepped in close. He put his arms around her and they both turned to Sheriff Harker.

Harker said to the shaggy guy at the counter, "Stop the movie and make an announcement. Tell everyone to get into their cars, roll up their windows, and leave the theater immediately."

"You want me to tell people to *leave* the theater?" Shaggy said. "You know how much trouble I'd get into for *that*?"

"You've *got* to. Those people are a *buffet* out there," Rodney said.

"Are you serious about this ... spider?" he said.

"Very serious," Harker said. "Evacuate the theater *now*."

"Dude," Rodney said, "I've *seen* the spider. I'm *dead* serious. Make the announcement or a lot of people are going to die. You want *that* to happen on your watch? What would the boss think if you let a bunch of people *die* in the theater?"

Shaggy thought about that for a moment, frowning as he chewed on his thumbnail. Finally, he nodded once and said, "Okay. I'll be right back."

He came out from behind the counter, walked across the snack bar to a door, and went through it.

"All right," Harker said, "I'm going out there. Stay in here till I come back."

He opened the door and walked out.

Rodney pulled away from Heidi, went to the open doorway, and looked outside. He could hear the ghostly sound of the movie's soundtrack coming from scores of car radios through rolled-down windows. Then it stopped, as did the movie on the screen, which went white. Silence fell over the drive-in for a moment. Then Rodney heard the announcement. It wasn't the counter guy's voice; it was someone older.

"Ladies and gentlemen, we ask that you get in your cars, roll up your windows, and leave the theater in an orderly fashion immediately. This is an emergency, and we are evacuating the theater. Please drive out in an orderly fashion. Thank you."

While the announcement was being made, the counter guy came back in, still holding the bat, but he said nothing.

Rodney and Heidi went over to the counter and leaned their hips on it. He took her hand and squeezed it. They waited.

Forty-Two

Marty Koenig hurried from his car to the small playground set up next to the snack bar. He hadn't been crazy about bringing their seven-year-old boy to a movie called *Thrill Killer*, but their babysitter had backed out on them at the last minute, so it was either bring little Danny along or stay home. He and his wife Cathy had needed a night out, and they both liked scary movies. They figured Danny would pay no attention to the screen as long as he was playing in the playground with other kids.

Marty had no idea why it might be necessary to evacuate the drive-in theater, but the use of the word made him very nervous. He automatically thought of terrorists, dirty bombs, and radiation sickness.

There were a couple tall lights shining over the playground, and Marty did not understand what he was seeing.

There were about half a dozen, maybe eight kids on the playground, but they were all lying on the ground.

Marty broke into a jog and closed the gap between himself and the playground. He stopped and looked down at the small bodies and tried to process what lay before him.

One of the boys was missing a leg, which lay a few feet away. Another lay beside his severed arm. One child was on her back, clothes torn, abdomen ripped wide open. They were bloody and lifeless, the children, and Marty found himself whimpering as he looked for Danny's familiar green sweater.

There he was, right over there by the foot of the slide.

"Oh, Jesus, Danny, oh, Jesus," he whimpered as he went over to his son.

Danny lay face down on the gravel. Marty bent down and gently clasped Danny's forearm and rolled him over onto his back.

The boy's head did not move when the body rolled—it stayed where it was, face down, the neck bloody and jagged.

Marty screamed then. It was high and sounded like a woman's scream. He dropped to his knees and his scream became wailing sobs.

Footsteps approached and he looked up to see Sheriff Harker. He recognized him because he'd seen him on the local news so many times. He had a shotgun tucked under his right arm.

"You okay?" Harker asked.

Marty shook his head and groaned, "No. No no no, I'm not okay."

Harker scanned the small playground and said, "Oh, fuck."

Forty-Three

Gary Boyle guzzled beer and smoked one cigarette after another as he watched *Thrill Killer* with his friends. He was with Ollie Peabo and Matt Parker in the back of Matt's pickup truck. Gary liked the smell of the popcorn from the snack bar and thought he'd probably get up and go get some pretty soon, but for now, he was content to stay put and watch the movie and drink beer.

They had graduated last year, but sometimes they still hung around the high school at the end of the day to talk to girls. Ollie looked the oldest—he *was* the oldest, having been held back two years in school—and had bought the beer. They went to a small liquor store in Newbury where a doddering old man ran the register in the evenings. He hardly looked at his customers as he sold them liquor, and he'd paid no attention to Ollie as he sold him a twelve-pack.

They had a boombox in the truck bed with them and listened to the movie on it as they drank their beer. They cheered on the movie's nudity and killings.

Somewhere in the drive-in, someone screamed.

Ollie laughed and said, "Somebody's gettin' off."

Matt pointed at the topless woman on the screen and said, "That girl's got tits just like Maryanne Trent."

"You never seen Maryanne Trent's tits," Gary said with a chuckle.

"Wanna bet?" Matt said. "Winter Festival, in the ball closets in the gym."

"You're so fulla shit," Ollie said.

"I am not!" Matt said. "She's got them really big ... whattaya call 'em? Oreos? Oreolas? Somethin' like that."

"Where'd the movie go?" Ollie said, frowning at the white screen.

Gary said, "Hey, didn't you guys hear what they just said over the radio? They're 'vacuating the theater."

"What?" Ollie said.

"Some guy just said they're 'vacuating the theater," Gary said again. "Look, people are leaving."

Matt turned and looked at the snack bar. "There's a buncha cop cars here, too," he said.

"What the hell's goin' on?" Ollie said.

"Well, I want popcorn before we leave," Gary said. "I been cravin' some, I just didn't wanna miss any of the movie." He got to his feet and went to the tailgate, jumped off. "I'll be right back."

"Get me some Red Vines," Ollie called.

Gary looked around on his way to the snack bar. Headlights were coming on and cars were heading for the front gate. He wondered what was going on. If he saw one of the cops, he'd ask.

He noticed the snack bar's door was closed. That seemed odd. There were also four sheriff's department cars parked around the small building, but he didn't see any deputies. Two deputies stood with a group of people, most of whom were crying, over in the small playground next to the snack bar.

He entered the snack bar and stood in the open doorway a moment.

Gary recognized Rodney Lepke, but he didn't know the girl. *Pretty fuckin' nice,* he thought as he quickly looked her over. Rodney and his friend stood against the counter. Behind them stood the guy who worked there at the counter. All three of them stared at him with big eyes.

He stood there and stared back a moment. Why were they looking at him like that? He waited, thinking they were going to say something to him, but they did not speak.

"What?" Gary said.

Something jumped on Gary from behind. He heard the girl scream as he was knocked hard to the floor on his face. He struggled to get up, but couldn't, then pain exploded in his back, deep burning pain, and he felt blood rise up in his throat, tasted it.

Gary was dead before he could utter a sound.

Forty-Four

Rodney and Heidi wasted no time in jumping over the orange counter. There was an open doorway behind the counter and Rodney went to it, pulling Heidi behind him by the hand. Shaggy headed there, too. The three of them collided outside the doorway.

The counter guy went in first, then Rodney and Heidi followed. Rodney turned and closed the door, but it wouldn't catch.

He looked down at the knob, but there was no knob. There was a hole in the door where the knob should be. The door would not close.

"Shit," Rodney said. He turned around and pressed his back to the door, holding it closed.

They were in a small storage room. A couple of brooms and a mop in a bucket leaned against the wall. There were big plastic bags of unpopped popcorn, packages of paper towels, stacked boxes of candy, boxes of napkins and straws. A bare bulb hung from the ceiling with a small chain attached.

"Let's hope it doesn't try to get in here," Rodney said, "because I don't know if I'll be able to hold it off for long."

Forty-Five

Harker heard the scream. As he followed the sound, he realized it had come from the snack bar. He looked over there and saw the door was open.

He'd been walking along rows of cars looking for the spider. Other deputies searched on foot, while some drove around the lot in their cruisers, which wasn't easy with everyone leaving all at once.

As he neared the snack bar, Harker saw a pair of feet sticking out of the doorway, toes down. He jogged the rest of the way.

A teenage boy lay in the doorway, a bloody hole in his back. Harker lifted his head and looked into the building.

The spider was on the other side of the snack bar, its back to him.

Harker stepped over the body into the snack bar, raised his shotgun, and called, "Rodney?"

A door behind the counter pulled open a bit and Rodney's face looked out.

"We're in here, Sheriff!" he shouted.

The spider turned around.

Harker fired and two of the spider's legs shattered. It charged forward unsteadily.

Harker racked the gun to fire again, but it was on him. He fell backward on top of the teenager's body.

"Rodney!" Harker shouted, his voice high with panic. He fired the gun and a hole appeared in the wall to Harker's left.

He felt the spider's fangs enter his abdomen. He thought of Rodney, and he threw the shotgun through the air, over the spider, and onto the floor across the room.

His last thought was of Anna, of kissing her.

Death came shortly after he heard the spider begin to eat him.

Forty-Six

Rodney pulled the door open a little more.

"Sheriff?" he called. He looked over his shoulder at Heidi and said, "Stay here."

"You're not going out there," she whispered. Her voice was tremulous, but very firm and decisive.

"I'll be right back."

Heidi made a small, inarticulate sound of protest in her throat as her brow furrowed deeply above her tense eyes.

Rodney stepped out of the storage room. He heard a sound that filled him with dread—wet slurping and smacking. He walked slowly and cautiously to the counter, placed his hands on the cold, flat surface.

The spider was on Sheriff Harker.

Rodney saw something on the floor peripherally and turned toward it. On the floor in front of the counter lay Harker's shotgun. He'd thrown it there for Rodney to get.

He looked at the spider again. It was eating the sheriff. The sounds it made were wet and thick.

Heart pounding, Rodney vaulted over the counter. He landed softly, not wanting to make any noise. The shotgun lay two feet away. He bent down, picked it up, and turned to face the spider.

At the same time, the crippled spider turned to face him.

Rodney raised the gun and it made a loud, satisfying sound as he racked it.

The spider, which was just inside the door, started toward him. It was wounded and did not move as fast as it had before, but it moved fast enough.

Rodney aimed at the hairy face, at those three black fangs. He squeezed the trigger, and the shotgun delivered a solid click.

It was empty.

Forty-Seven

Deputy Kevin Lomander walked away from the group of sobbing, traumatized parents who were finding their small children in pieces in the playground. He had to get away, if only for a moment. He was a parent, too. He and his wife had a two-year-old, little Tammy, and he felt for those parents. Maybe he felt a little too much—he'd been at this for only a year, and he had not yet hardened himself to all the pain he encountered in his job.

His mouth was dry as a bone—he could hardly swallow. Kevin headed for the snack bar to get something to drink. He saw the two feet in the doorway and ran the rest of the way.

"Sheriff?" he said when he recognized the sheriff lying on top of another guy. Kevin made a strangled sound in his throat when he saw the big hole in the center of Sheriff Harker. He saw the spider just a few feet away. Its back was to Kevin and it was just starting to move forward. Kevin saw the young man holding the shotgun—he looked shocked and terrified.

Kevin racked his shotgun and put it to his shoulder.

Forty-Eight

Rodney was paralyzed. The shotgun was empty, he had no weapon. And even though it was wounded, the spider was still fast enough to keep him from getting over the counter.

It was getting closer and Rodney was so scared that when he tried to cry out, his dry throat only made a cracked, broken sound. He held the gun out before him, and the spider got close enough to close its fangs on the barrel.

Rodney shoved the shotgun farther into the spider's mouth, and it backed up a little. He pushed harder, and the spider moved back farther.

Before he could push again, the spider's left front leg swung up and easily knocked the gun from his hands. It clattered over the floor as it slid away from Rodney. Somehow, he felt even worse without it, even though the shotgun was empty and useless. At least it had allowed him to hold off the spider for a few seconds. Now he had nothing.

The spider started forward again and there was an explosion in the small snack bar. The rear part of the spider's abdomen exploded and splattered a white gooey substance in all directions. It was warm on Rodney's face as it dribbled down his cheeks.

The spider lay flat on the floor, dead.

Rodney found he could not move, except for the rise and fall of his chest as he gasped for breath. He stared down at the spider, at the bloody fangs now with tiny bits of flesh caught on the serrations. The two small eyes remained perched atop the head, black and as dead in death as they had been in life. One of them had been broken open and leaked a white viscera.

Hands closed on his arm and he turned with a gasp to find Heidi at his side. She pulled him away from the spider and embraced him. She had a napkin in her hand and she used it to wipe his face. She was speaking, but Rodney could not understand her. His ears rang loudly from the gunshot, which had been like a bomb going off in the snack bar.

The deputy who'd fired the shotgun stood just inside the door, his mouth open as he breathed hard, staring with wide eyes at the dead spider.

Rodney looked down at the spider. Heidi put her arm around his shoulders and he put his arms around her waist.

The spider began to melt.

Rodney frowned and tilted his head forward as he watched it melt into a puddle that spread over the floor.

"Rodney, what's happening?" Heidi said.

As the puddle grew and neared their shoes, Rodney realized the spider had not melted—it was now a clearer, brighter yellow and still perfectly solid.

Rodney and Heidi stumbled backward together as Heidi screamed and Rodney said, "Shit, they're *babies*!" He started stomping his feet on the small spiders.

They spread out on the snack bar floor in a cloud of tiny pumping legs and little black fangs.

"Son of a *bitch*!" the deputy shouted as he turned and stepped back over the two bodies on the floor and went out the door.

Heidi climbed up on the counter.

Rodney kept stepping on them, but he was not fast enough. Two of the spiders, each a couple inches long, crawled up his sock to his shin. He cried out when one of them bit him. But he didn't have time to tend to it because they kept coming.

"This way!" Shaggy shouted. He came out from behind the counter and ran across the room to the doorway on the other side.

Rodney and Heidi followed as he opened the door and went through. The baby spiders crunched faintly beneath their feet. Once they'd passed through the door, Shaggy slammed it.

"This goes to the projection shack," he said. "We can get out through there."

They went down a short hall to another door and into the projection shack. It was empty and dark.

"Looks like Chuck took off already," Shaggy said.

Rodney stopped, rolled up the leg of his jeans and slapped the spiders off his leg, then stepped on them. There were two bites, and they were very painful and bleeding. Rodney clenched his teeth as he stood upright again.

Shaggy went out the door on the other side of the small room.

Rodney took Heidi's hand and said, "Come on, let's get the hell out of here."

About the Author

Ray Garton has been writing novels, novellas, short stories, and essays for more than 30 years. His work spans the genres of horror, crime, suspense, and even comedy. *Live Girls* was nominated for the Bram Stoker Award in 1988, and Garton received the Grand Master of Horror Award at the 2006 World Horror Convention. He lives in northern California with his wife Dawn, where he is at work on a new novel.

BIBLIOGRAPHY

NOVELS AND NOVELLAS

411
Bestial
Biofire
Crawlers
Crucifax
Dark Channel

Darklings
Live Girls
Lot Lizards
Loveless
Night Life
Meds
Murder Was My Alibi
Ravenous
Scissors
Seductions
Serpent Girl
Sex and Violence in Hollywood
Shackled
The Folks
The Folks 2
The Loveliest Dead
The Man in the Palace Theater
The New Neighbor
Trade Secrets
Trailer Park Noir
Vortex
Zombie Love

COLLECTIONS

Methods of Madness
'Nids And Other Stories
Pieces of Hate
Slivers of Bone
The Disappeared and Other Stories
The Girl in the Basement and Other Stories
Wailing and Gnashing of Teeth

CROSSROAD
PRESS

www.ingramcontent.com/pod-product-compliance
Lightning Source LLC
LaVergne TN
LVHW090950080826
845145LV00003B/953

* 9 7 8 1 6 3 7 8 9 6 7 0 9 *